The House on Bristol Street

SHIRLEY WIGGINS

NEWMAN SPRINGS PUBLISHING
320 Broad Street
Red Bank, NJ 07701

First originally published by Newman Springs Publishing 2020

ISBN 978-1-64801-625-7 (Paperback)
ISBN 978-1-64801-626-4 (Digital)

Printed in the United States of America

For the strong women in my life. Katrina, Ryce, Mary, Kathy and Susie. You've made all the difference.

Prologue

Cate still couldn't believe she had been lucky enough to purchase this house. She walked from room to room, marveling and imagining how it would be to have people living within these walls, to hear voices and laughter around her. She was lonely, and it was a beautiful old house, with lots of bedrooms to house the kids she hoped to one day bring inside. Right now, it needed a little work. Gallons of fresh paint, some elbow grease, and a lot of love would do wonders for the place; but the bones were good...really good, and the mechanicals were sound. The furnace was nearly new, as was the air and the hot water heater. The roof was only two years old, and the plumbing and electrical had recently been updated. On the inside were the charming details that made this house shine for Cate. Crown molding added to the depth of the high ceilings. There were two beautiful fireplaces with custom carpentry mantels from years ago, maybe even the last century, that Gabe, the previous owner, had diligently brought back to its original beauty. One was in the living room and, the other, in the dining room. The skills necessary for the detail of the woodwork in this house were rare today, and she felt so fortunate to be able to save it for future generations to appreciate.

Her favorite room in the house was the kitchen. It was old and new at the same time. On the window wall were abundant shelves where upper cupboards used to be, and they appeared to be made of old barn wood. She could envision all of her much loved cobalt blue Fiesta ware displayed upon them. She relished the idea of leaving them out on open shelves so she could actually see what she had and find it when she needed it. That would be a nice change from the tiny beach house where she had to nearly empty a cabinet completely in order to locate a specific item.

The appliances were updated but looked as though they belonged in an old house, and it had all the space and conveniences for preparing wonderful meals. Under the double window, a deep farm sink was flanked on either side with light quartz countertops. Opposite the sink stood a big butcher block island ideal for prep work and extra seating when called for. Over on the right was a butler's pantry that would house all of the small appliances that she collected. She reveled in the art of cooking and serving people the food she prepared, which explained why she was a sucker for kitchen gadgets. It was going to be a real change to have enough space to store everything out of sight.

She was new to Middleton, and it simply had to have been a miracle that she found this house. After all, it wasn't even on the market.

CHAPTER 1

A Time for Change

As Cate walked the neighborhood, getting to know the area around her, she passed quaint shops, small businesses, and neat little homes with well-tended yards. The city plans included plenty of green spaces as well. Miles of walking and bike riding trails were available, and her favorite, so far, was in the Pheasant Branch Conservatory. It was shaded by huge trees and incorporated views of prairie and wildlife. It boasted man-made bridges and neat wooden paths. Walking along the trails, one could glimpse small ponds, and showcased on a hillside was a panoramic view of a sunflower field. Benches were scattered around, and most brandished little plaques dedicated to loved ones long gone. The trails were wide enough for walkers and bikers alike, and they were well tended. She could lose herself for hours there, with only the music from her iPhone to keep her company.

Cate felt she had found the best of both worlds in Middleton—city and small town. She first came here because she had read about it in a "best places to live" magazine article. She was usually a warm-weather girl, but her life had just changed so drastically since she lost David, and she was badly in need of something new, something out of her comfort zone. Middleton, Wisconsin, had a small-town friendly atmosphere that made her feel safe and comfortable, the way she had felt as a child growing up in North Carolina.

Just a few miles down the road was Madison, a vibrant college town rich in culture and ripe with enthusiasm. Paraded on downtown streets were museums, theaters, music venues, and restaurants of every flavor. Loyal and vocal Badger sports fans of the university were sporting red and white everywhere they went. There was so much to enjoy and so much to keep one's mind occupied.

She had been hired in Madison at the University Hospital in the respiratory therapy department, but she had a month off before she started. She was only going back to work part-time to keep her skills sharp and because she enjoyed patient care. She often got close to her patients, and they, to her. She didn't need the income anymore. David had seen to that. Between the insurance settlement and careful investing, she was going to be just fine in the money department. Sometimes, she wondered how in the world she was going to continue on without him.

Cate walked by an interesting local bakery every day. She was exploring new places in town and had wandered into the shop for a coffee and pastry early on a Thursday morning, when the shop was nearly empty of customers. As she looked around, she instantly felt at home in the little shop. There were only about eight tables, all covered with white linen tablecloths and small intricate candle centerpieces. The walls were covered with photography from a local artist. They were mostly nature shots, but there was a striking portrait of a man and woman laughing. They looked very much in love, and it was positioned in a prominent place on the wall, by the display case, so that everyone could see it. On a little wooden table beside the portrait stood a stack of business cards, "Photos by Katrina," and some pieces were for sale. She took a card and placed it in her purse for future reference. Turning her attention to the bakery items, she looked through the sparkling glass case to find mouthwatering displays of cookies, bars, savory and sweet breads, cakes, and pies. Cate could tell just by looking around that the place was well taken care of and that it must be owned by someone invested in their work. She chose a table where she could study the portrait and sat down. It was a wonderful little place and just sitting at the table made her feel quite comfortable and relaxed.

Contemplating the photo, she realized that it reminded her of herself and David. She had been really lucky in her relationship with him. They'd met in college in a microbiology course. They had been assigned to each other as lab partners by their professor. It turned out to be a happy accident that changed her life forever, and she was still grateful for that. Camaraderie dominated the relationship for nearly two years before they became romantically involved because they both valued the easy friendship they shared, and they were each hesitant to risk it. They reveled in each other's company. Compatibility and affection kindled the fire of their mutual affection. David was the kindest man she had ever known. He was eternally optimistic and upbeat. He saw the good in everyone he met, and he brought out the positive in her. Everyone he met considered him a friend, and he was comfortable in the company of both men and women. She tended to be more reserved and less trusting than he. She was contemplative and quiet, and he, passionate and boisterous. She was judgmental upon first impression and slow to reevaluate once an opinion was formed. They shared many interests in common and could converse on many topics. They were each opinionated but could argue their points easily, all in good fun, without temper or malice. They were yin and yang. He would call her on her stubbornness and encourage her to see things from a different perspective when she judged people too harshly. She respected and valued his opinions. She could keep him grounded when he lost himself in dreamland, and for some reason she could not fathom, he was completely devoted to her. She was a better person with him in her life, and she missed him so much that, at times, getting through her day was a challenge she only managed because she knew that he would want her to.

Moments later, Mrs. Miles came over to Cate's table to take her order. She smiled, introduced herself as baker, bottle washer and proprietor of Hannah's Bakery. It was too late for the before-work crowd and too early for the lunch rush, so the place only had one other customer. Cate complimented her on the atmosphere of the place. She ordered a black coffee and an apple pastry. Hannah breezed off to get the coffee pot, leaving Cate alone with her thoughts. She studied the portrait again and noticed that the woman in the photo must be the woman that was waiting on her. She was definitely younger in the photo, but it had to be her. She possessed the same affectionate dimpled grin and the same stunning blue eyes.

Hannah promptly returned with a delicate apple pastry and a steaming pot of coffee. She poured some in a big ceramic mug, put down the sugar and creamer, and placed the pastry on the table in front of Cate, while asking if there was anything thing else she could get for her. Cate asked her about the photo; Hannah looked up at it and smiled.

She said, "Yes...that is a favorite of mine. It's a picture of me and my husband, Gabe, almost twenty years ago. We were the best of friends, and this was taken at our cottage up north in Eagle River by the photographer whose work is exhibited here in my shop. Gabe is gone now, and every time I look at that picture, I remember how happy we were and how incredibly blessed I was to have him in my life." Hannah smiled down at Cate again, excused herself, and went over to check on her other customer. *So*, Cate thought, *no wonder it reminds me of David.*

Cate started coming into the little bakery several mornings a week for breakfast. Hannah was always there in the mornings, and she and Cate had fallen into easy conversation, even though the woman was probably almost twice her age. "Please call me Hannah," she said, and they soon discovered that they shared a lot in common—a love of food, books, gardening, and now, they both found themselves alone. Cate mentioned that she was new to the area but that she had fallen in love with Middleton, and she was currently looking for a more permanent place to live. For the moment, she was happily ensconced in a tiny apartment off of University Avenue.

Hannah had noticed that Cate always came in alone. She was curious about her. *She wasn't a classic beauty*, Hannah thought to herself. *She would probably be considered a pretty girl.* She looked healthy and natural. She had honey-colored hair that fell well below her shoulders, with little spiral curls at the ends. Her eyes were large, brown, and very expressive, with thick dark lashes. And when she listened to Hannah speak, there was a little crease in her brow that showed she was invested and interested in the conversation. Her skin was lovely, clear, bright, and fresh. She wore little, if any, makeup.

Her face was always pink with color, and Hannah thought it was because she seemed to prefer to walk everywhere rather than travel by car. She preferred casual clothes and frequently wore jeans and tees, her feet encased in running shoes. She had a compact, fit little form and couldn't have weighed much over 120 pounds. She appeared to be in her mid to late twenties, but then, appearances could be deceiving. Hannah wanted to know her better. She and Gabe had no children, and she felt a strange sort of maternal instinct about her new little customer. Hannah wanted to make sure that she found her way around and that she had someone that cared enough to check to see if she was okay.

One day, when Cate was in the bakery, Hannah suggested they go out to try some of the restaurants in Madison to help her get to know her new home a little better. Cate quickly agreed. She would love to have some company at dinner, and she was very interested in getting to know Hannah away from her work. She wanted to share some quality conversation when there were no customers to check in on. Hannah suggested that they meet the next day at 6:30 p.m. at Harvest.

"This place is incredible," Hannah said. "They source local farms and produce, so the menu is always fresh. I think you'll like it."

Hannah was already seated at a table when Cate arrived. As she approached, her gait was steady and confident, and Hannah felt happy to see her. She sat down in front of Hannah, pushed her long hair back and smiled.

"I really appreciate the invitation. I haven't been to this place before, and it sure smells good in here."

Just then, a young brunette stopped in front of their table, "Hi, I'm Brittany, and I'll be your server today. Can I get you girls something to drink?"

Hannah and Cate each ordered water and looked over the menu.

"So," asked Hannah, "what brings you to Middleton?" Cate looked at Hannah, considered keeping the details to herself, but she liked Hannah and so decided to be upfront about her situation. She was lonely and relished having a friend in this new town.

"My husband David and I lived in Wilmington, North Carolina. We had a little place right on the water. Last fall, David was killed in a car crash when someone crossed the center line and took the best friend I had in the world out of my life. I tried to carry on in that house, but everything reminded me of what I'd lost. I felt frozen in time. Couldn't move forward, and I couldn't go back. David was the only family I had. He was my love, my life, my husband. I needed to get away from that beach house. I took out a map, laid it open on the table, closed my eyes, and pointed to it. When I opened my eyes, my finger was on Wisconsin. Not long after that, I came across an article in *US News and World report* entitled "50 best places to live in the US." Middleton was number one on the list. I took it as a sign. I sold my house, quit my job, packed up or gave away all of my belongings, and started my new journey to Middleton. I've only been here three weeks, but I've fallen in love with the feel of it and want to make it a more permanent arrangement. I'm a little nervous about winter. The winters in North Carolina are milder and much shorter. Perhaps, I should find a realtor and start looking for a house."

Hannah was heartbroken for her new young friend. Brittany arrived back at the table to bring their water and take their order.

"I think I'll try the squash soup and a side salad please," said Cate.

"That sounds good. I'll have the same," Hannah replied absentmindedly.

Once Brittany had bounded off to help another customer, Hannah said, "My Gabe got sick." Cate looked at her, and it seemed that she was miles away as she spoke. "He was always so vital, so alive! He didn't want to get out of bed one morning. We both thought it was a flu bug. When we finally went in to the doctor, they ran some blood test and admitted him to stay overnight in the hospital for observation. He was experiencing nausea and vomiting, and next, he started to lose so much weight. He developed a yellowish skin color—even his eyes appeared yellow. We never came home again together. He was diagnosed with pancreatic cancer. It took him quickly. He was in a lot of pain in the end, and I was so torn over his suffering and my need to keep him close to me that I couldn't cope. I was struggling, and I guess, if truth be told, I still am. I miss him. He was so clever and funny. We were extremely close. One of his passions was European history. He taught over at the University in Madison for twenty-five years. You would have liked him. Everybody did. He possessed a melodic British accent that could make me swoon, and when he smiled, it was perceptible all the way to his eyes.

"He also reveled in another love, and when he was taken ill, he had been refurbishing an old two-story house over on Bristol Street. He was having the time of his life. It was a labor of love for him, and he was so careful about every little detail. He wanted us to live there when it was finished. He referred to it as his love story to me."

Her eyes welled with tears, and Cate thought she could actually feel Hannah's pain. It was a raw and feral thing. The empathy rose up like bile, and Cate's memory of losing David was as strong as if it had just happened yesterday. She thought, *What a thing to bond over, considering we have both suffered such similar loss in our lives. It's no wonder we get along so well.* Her thoughts were interrupted by Brittany bringing their food to the table. The soup was splendid, and as they finished their meal, they were both deep in thought. Cate was brought back to the present by Brittany asking if they would care for anything else. They split the check and said their goodbyes.

Hannah thought about Cate's story all the way home. It pained her that Cate, at such a young age, had experienced the sudden death of her husband. Would moving across country by herself help her to outrun her memories? She must be in possession of a great deal of fortitude. Her thoughts drifted to the Bristol Street house…maybe she should show it to Cate. It was sitting empty, and Gabe wouldn't have liked that. She had only been back to the house a couple of times since his death, and she knew that even though he loved this house, she would never be able to live in it without him. It still needed a good deal of work. Would Cate even be interested? Was it too much for her to take on? There was only one way to find out.

Cate was also thinking of Hannah on her way home. She was such an interesting woman. Cate had no family other than David, and now he was gone too. She felt a real fondness for Hannah, a kinship that was lacking in her life and was really glad that she had opted to enter the little bakery that day. Meeting Hannah had felt, to Cate, like serendipity or providence.

CHAPTER 2

A Little Hard Work

Cate stopped into Hannah's the next morning for breakfast. She ordered a croissant and black coffee and was thanking Hannah again for inviting her to dinner the night before when Hannah asked if she would like to see the Bristol Street house Gabe had been working on. She said that as much as Gabe loved it, at this point, she couldn't bring herself to finish the project. Cate was intrigued. Hannah told her that Gabe had stripped the house to the studs. The electrical and plumbing were both redone. He had reroofed, dry walled, and had refurbished the three bathrooms. The kitchen was completely remodeled. The place was still in disarray and needed someone unafraid of hard work to get in there to clean and paint. Floors still needed to be refinished, but they were original heart of pine and would be lovely when they were resurfaced.

Hannah realized that she was excited to show Cate the house. Maybe this could be an answer for both of them. Hannah hated the fact that the house was sitting empty, but she didn't want just anyone to live in it. She thought Gabe would have hated it too. Cate needed a place to live. If this house suited her, maybe Gabe was watching over them both. It seemed like a reasonable solution. Hannah drew a map on a napkin and handed it to Cate. They planned to meet the following afternoon at three in front of the house.

Cate was so excited when she reached the house. It was a rather large house. Maybe it was too big for her alone. What would one person do with all that space? It had a covered porch, and Cate imagined a couple of rockers on it and some ferns hanging from the eaves. The windows on the facade were long and shuttered, and Cate thought that they may reach nearly to the floor on the inside. Extending toward the front of the lawn were a couple of evergreens and a pretty little walkway of paver stones that curved and wound up toward the house. Hostas lined either side of the pavers. Featured at the entry was a big hickory wood front door, with bold black hardware. A little wrought iron fence encompassed the whole of the front yard. Cate envisioned a Dickens novel, and she was bursting to see the inside.

As was her habit, she was early. She paced up and down in front of the white house, taking in every detail. She was enchanted. Pacing helped her pass the time, but it also allowed her to admire the prospect of the property from every angle. She had her back to the house observing the neighborhood when she heard Hannah call her name. She turned and walked back up the walkway to where Hannah was now standing. She quivered in anticipation. This house was beckoning to her.

"Well, now," said Hannah mischievously, "shall we look inside?"

Cate looked around upon entering the house. She entered into a foyer with a coat closet on one side and, on the other, stood a bench flanked with shelving that Gabe had designed. He had placed hooks above the bench for storing scarves, hats, and mittens when entering in winter. There was a place for everything. It was a thoughtful and attractive design. Just past the entry, the house was constructed in a foursquare design, in which the living room was on one side of the hallway and the dining room was on the other. The kitchen was located in the back past the dining room, and there was a room just beyond the living room with French doors that Cate thought would be perfect for an office. A beautiful winding staircase with a curved wooden banister led up to the bedrooms. A walk-up unfinished attic space encompassed the whole of the third floor, and the heavy duty-door possessed a massive black metal lock in which a key was inserted. *This would be an excellent storage area, and it's so great that the key is right here and actually locks the door*, she thought. She left the key in the door and then she turned to descend the stairs. As she neared the living room again, she noted that the windows were just as she had surmised from the outside of the house. They reached from eight inches below the ceiling to a foot above floor, with the ceilings being twelve feet high, and they really showcased the yard with the evergreens on the front lawn. Cate could only imagine how beautiful this yard would be covered in snow. She pictured big holiday meals in the spacious dining room. She was mentally placing furniture around in the rooms. What could she say? She was in love with this house! She saw all the work that needed to be completed, but she wasn't daunted. This house was perfect in her mind. She advanced into the kitchen and thought it couldn't have been more suited to her taste if she had designed it herself. Additionally, there were four nice-sized bedrooms and two and a half baths. She wasn't sure what she would do with all this room, but if Hannah was willing to sell, she was most assuredly buying.

As soon as the keys were in her hands, Cate got to work. She hired a professional that Hannah had recommended to refinish all the floors, and he agreed to start the next week. She planned to take care of everything else herself. Gabe had really done a thorough job refurbishing the place. The details were incredible, and Cate was still noticing small touches he had added that she had not noticed before. Many of the built-ins and trim pieces Cate had thought were original to the house turned out to be Gabe's handiwork. He had simply done such a skillful job that she couldn't tell the difference until she got close enough to paint the detail work. What a talent he had and how lucky was she to have been offered this place!

She had returned to work the previous week, but she was only covering sixteen to twenty hours a week, and her schedule was flexible. Every spare minute aside from work and sleep, she put into the house. First, she tackled the painting. It was a monumental task because of the size of the place and because Cate was so meticulous. She wanted everything painted before the floors were done so that she wouldn't damage them with paint spatter. A massive amount of exquisite trim needed to be stained, and as daunting a task as it was, she rose to the occasion. In the end, the result was breathtaking.

Hannah had been a godsend, showing Cate around the area. She got recommendations from some of her customers for the capable workmen to refinish the floors. She had recommended the best shops.

"Brennan's has the best produce, and you can taste test everything. They put out little sample cups and toothpicks especially for that purpose. Who wants to get home only to discover the apples you just purchased are mealy? Jacobson Bros. sells potato salad that is so good I don't even make my own anymore." She told her where her polling place would be since Election Day was nearing. Hannah had even researched bus schedules to help Cate navigate her route to work without having to drive.

Cate had not yet moved in and was still living out of her tiny apartment. The few things that Cate had kept sat in a storage unit until her new home repairs were complete. Hannah arrived carrying a pot of soup and some bowls and spoons one day; on another, it was a bottle of wine and glasses. On a couple of occasions, after she had closed her shop for the day, Hannah packed up some pastries and coffee and showed up at Cate's door to help her clean, paint, or anything else that needed to be done.

One evening, Cate sat sipping a cup of coffee while she took a break from polishing the stairway banister, and she found herself watching Hannah washing the windows in the dining room. Again, she felt that there had to be someone watching over her to have brought such a treasure into her life and at this time in her life when she was in so much pain and so alone. Cate didn't mind the work at all; as a matter of fact, she thrived on it and would gladly have finished everything alone, but it had been so much easier and so much more enjoyable with Hannah here. She watched as Hannah stretched to try to reach the length of the window.

Hannah was tall at five feet eight and about twenty pounds overweight; what she liked to call "fluffy." She possessed bright startling-blue eyes and an impish grin, with dimples on both cheeks. She had small incredibly white teeth that made her smile even more remarkable. She was only forty-seven, but the shock of white hair on her head had been white as snow for over ten years already. She was bright and sensitive and had a razor-sharp wit paired with a kind heart, and Cate found so much to be grateful for in her. The friendship, this house, their trips around town to discover the area, sitting at a table drinking coffee, and sharing their troubles and triumphs— all of this was like some kind of therapy, and Cate was beginning to feel that she was among the living again. She had come to consider Hannah family. They couldn't have been closer had they been sisters, and even though she couldn't have known, Hannah felt exactly the same way.

As Cate watched Hannah, she began to laugh. "Hey," she smirked, "I know you've got some height on your side, but even you are not going to be able to reach the top of those windows without a stool."

Hannah looked up and smiled. "Let's call it a day. I'll bring a stool from the shop tomorrow. I think we only have another day or two, and we'll be ready to start moving your things in. Do you have enough furniture to fill this house?"

Cate grinned. "How do you feel about yard sales and thrift shops?" she asked.

At last, the house was finished, and it had turned out beautifully. The floors were absolutely gorgeous, and Cate was still pinching herself to make sure it wasn't a dream. She walked from room to room, taking in every detail.

The movers had brought her things in, and box upon box was waiting to be unpacked and organized. She valued good quality linens and opened several boxes filled with pieces that she had accumulated during her years with David. With three bathrooms and four bedrooms in this house, she was suddenly very glad she had brought all of it. The kitchen items filled at least four more boxes, and she wasn't entirely sure what could be hidden in the others, but she was excited to have accomplished so much and to be able to unpack and have some of her things displayed around her. The only furniture she had brought was the much beloved king-size bed she had shared with David, which the movers had set up in one of the bedrooms upstairs, two roomy cream-colored club chairs with nailhead trim, and a few random tables and lamps. Her beach house had been really small, and many of the items that filled it had been sold or given away to friends before she left Wilmington.

She was definitely going to have to do some furniture shopping. Right now, as long as she had a bed and a couple of chairs, she would be fine here. There was no dining room furniture, but she'd borrowed a couple of stools from Hannah that slid right up to the island in the kitchen, and that would suffice. She could pick up other pieces as she found things she liked.

Cate tackled the kitchen first. She could hardly wait to prepare some home-cooked cuisine and wanted everything to be in its place. How had she ever gotten so much stuff squeezed into that tiny kitchen at the beach house? The butler's pantry was filling up fast. Food processor, blender, Crockpot, waffle iron, serving bowls, and platters competed for space on the freshly painted wooden shelves. Big glass storage jars contained pastas, cereals, flour, sugar, and other baking goods lined across two long shelves. Which box contained her label maker? It certainly would help to keep things neat and organized. Opening the next box, she discovered her Fiesta ware collection. She cherished these sturdy bright-blue pieces. David had given her a piece to observe each Christmas and birthday they celebrated together because he knew how much she loved them. She was looking forward to arranging these pieces on the open shelving in the kitchen, along with the remaining white stoneware. They were durable, and she could match them with anything when she was entertaining company. When she was done with the kitchen, she climbed the stairs, showered, and headed off to sleep in her own bed. What a pleasure! She would not soon forget to be thankful for that.

Cate was settling into her new routine. Her days were filled in a more normal pace. She was enjoying her new job taking care of patients with all manner of illness. Her shifts were kept busy by administering treatments. She gave nebulizer treatments to people to ease airway constriction problems and taught patients with asthma how to use their newly prescribed inhalers and how to assess their own breathing patterns and triggers in order to recognize when they were experiencing more serious problems. She utilized cough assist devices to help patients that were unable to cough on their own to clear their lungs, CPAP machines were set up, five-minute walks were monitored in order to assess if patients needed oxygen for home use.

She worked with general care patients and with critical care patients breathing with the help of ventilators. She treated the old and the young and every age in between. She was passionate about her work, and her goal was to always leave her patients with a better outcome because of the care she took in evaluating and treating them. Because of the nature of lung disease, many of her patients were regulars, and she was already getting to know and care for them.

Even though she only worked two, sometimes three, days a week, her days were full. She enjoyed shopping for more pieces to complete each room. She was so excited to discover an old double-bed frame and chest at a garage sale a few blocks from her home. It was pretty banged up, and she couldn't have told anyone why she wanted it so badly, for she still didn't even have a sofa, but she paid twenty-five dollars for the two pieces and then paid two of the kids that lived there to pack it up and deliver it her house. They hauled the old pieces up the stairs and positioned them in the largest of the unclaimed bedrooms. Cate sanded them and painted them white. The low poster bed with spires on each of the posts stood regally by the window. She had painted this room a pale sunny yellow, and being in here with the sun dappling on the walls made her feel warm and happy. She bought a new mattress and box spring and found a yellow-and-white bedspread and curtains in her linen closet that would suit the purpose. She placed a very soft white rug on the floor and a table and lamp on each side of the bed. It was still sparse, but as she looked around the room at her handiwork, she was pleased with the results. The room was adorable. All she needed was a little something for the walls. Maybe she should get in touch with that artist friend of Hannah's.

CHAPTER 3

A Growing Friendship

Grace, one of Hannah's employees, was going to open the shop for her tomorrow. She usually worked a few hours in the afternoons, but she had a big trip coming up with her classmates for school and wanted to earn a little extra money. She was a junior at Middleton High school and had proven herself to be a level-headed, responsible girl. Hannah was glad to have her and had agreed to let her cover the whole day. Michael, a bakery student from the local tech school, worked four days a week for school credit. He did much of the baking now using Hannah's recipes, and he learned quickly. Hannah thought that he would be a fine addition to any bakery and could probably manage the desserts in one of the fancier restaurants in Madison if given the chance. The bakery was only open from 6:00 a.m. until 2:30 p.m., Monday through Saturday.

Hannah didn't take many days off out of habit. She had thrown herself into the business after Gabe died just to keep her sanity, but the truth was that she wasn't really needed to keep the place running smoothly. The kids did a great job and could be trusted to capably run the place. Hannah was a fixture. The customers had come to know her and liked to come in and chat, catch up on what was going on in the community. They would talk about local news, politics, and sports. They came in for the atmosphere, but they also came in to see Hannah. The fact that her pastries were divine and she served the tastiest fresh ground coffee didn't hurt either. Now she had two days in a row to do whatever she liked. Hannah's was her business, her pride and joy, and she took pleasure in being in the shop, but it had been too long since she took a whole weekend for herself. The bank deposit could wait until Monday.

Hannah was expected around seven. Cate was making a vegetable quiche for breakfast, and after that, they were going to start the day with a long walk in Pheasant Branch. The rest of the day was open for wherever the wind blew. They had no plans and no schedules to keep, and they were both looking forward to the promise of a great day. At just that moment, Cate heard a knock on the door and called out, "It's open...come on in."

Feeling a chill in the air, Hannah dressed in sweats and a hoodie. She wore a T-shirt underneath in case the weather warmed later in the day. She was well aware that Wisconsin weather was as changeable as a teenager. Her white hair atop her head was wild from having been whipped around by the wind. Her cheeks were pink, and her eyes were bright. She looked happy and energetic, and it was contagious.

"My goodness," said Cate, "what are you so happy about this morning?"

"I haven't had a whole weekend to myself for over a year," she answered. "What's on our agenda for today? I know you still need a sofa and a dining room table. Do you think we should try some secondhand stores, or should we search for estate sales in the paper? That could be fun. I hooked the little trailer up to my car, in case we find something that catches your eye."

"That's a great idea." Cate put a plate down on the island in front of Hannah. "Juice or coffee?" she asked. "Those are two pieces I really need and it'd be great to mark them off my list!" She exclaimed excitedly.

"Wow! This quiche is great! What did you put in it?" She was making little moaning noises as she chewed. "Um...um...and I'll have a cup of coffee please."

"Let's see, there's portabellas, spinach, cheddar, Gouda...a little salt, pepper, and a touch of cayenne, oh, and eggs of course! It's not exactly good for the waistline. I guess it's a good thing we're going to get a walk in this morning. Did you see a paper outside? Let's try an estate sale. I've never been to one before."

They walked five miles chattering and laughing like schoolgirls. The trail was busy with joggers and bikers and people strolling today. They passed several neighbors along the way. There must be something in the air; it seemed that everyone was in a good mood, smiling and waving. They came upon a couple that frequented the bakery, out walking their dogs, an adorable pair of Westies that answered to the names Sophie and Silas. The pups were happily strutting along with their masters, unhindered by their short little legs.

"It's great to see you somewhere besides work," called the man, Jack, to Hannah. "You should get out more often." Jack winked and waved, and before Hannah could blink, he and his wife had disappeared around the curved path, Sophie and Silas trotting along contentedly ahead of them.

Once they settled into the car, Cate and Hannah opened the paper to the advertisement section and promptly located ads for three estate sales. They chose one that was a few miles out in the country. It took about half an hour to negotiate the country road. The day warmed up as the sun blazed down on the hood of the car. Cate had taken off her jacket, and Hannah had removed her hoodie. The radio was blasting an old Led Zeppelin tune, and Hannah was singing at the top of her lungs. Hannah's window was full down, and the countryside was a sight to behold. Leaves hung on to trees, announcing the arrival of autumn with glorious reds, russets, and coppers. They felt revitalized from both their long walk and the beauty of the day. They turned down a winding drive toward an old gray farmhouse. A barn on a hill behind the house had seen better days. It was dilapidated, and the roof was sagging inward like it would fall at any moment. The whole place just appeared sad and tired. This was the second day of the sale, and it seemed that anything worth buying was already gone or marked as sold. Hannah and Cate were looking around half-heartedly when Cate squealed, scaring Hannah to death.

"There it is!" she pointed and squealed again. "Over there!" She pointed to an ill-used and forlorn old farm table. It was perfect, and there were eight chairs, one with arms! Cate lifted the tag and was delighted to discover the table and chair set cost forty dollars. Cate quickly scooped up the tag, without even negotiating, and paid what she considered a pittance. They maneuvered the whole set into the little trailer and progressed on down the drive in the same direction they had come.

"Are you sure you saw what I saw?" asked Hannah incredulously. "There were scars and scrapes all over that table...*and the chairs*!" She shook her head as if she couldn't quite believe the purchase. "The house it came out of was badly in need of some soap and water. Good grief, we can get you a new one."

"No, Hannah! I promise you it's perfect. You'll see, although I think you are right about the chairs. They are sturdy, and there are eight of them, but they will have to be painted. I'll either paint them white, or if I can match the paint, cobalt blue. It's going to look delightful. Trust me. The table is large enough to entertain...and eight chairs, all for the low, low price of forty dollars. I'm stoked!" With that, Cate had found herself another project.

When they got back to the house, they unloaded the set of table and chairs into the garage until such time as Cate could work her magic on it.

It was now nearly noon, and they had worked up an appetite hauling all that furniture around. They decided to just hit the drive through at Culver's for a burger. *There is just nothing in the world like a butter burger*, Cate thought as she took another big bite of the sandwich.

They scoured secondhand shops and thrift stores, but Cate couldn't find a sofa that suited her. She was either going to have to buy a new one or get something with good bones and reupholster it herself, something that she had not yet done and was hesitant to try. Well, it wasn't like she even had enough company over to use a sofa; she still had time to search. It would have been nice to know that she was finished with the house, but that was the final big purchase, and it could wait.

"Thank you for running all over town with me today," Cate said gratefully. "You have been an angel helping me pull the house together. Whatever would I have done without you?" She gave Hannah a big smile and hugged her appreciatively.

Hannah shrugged. "I think we have helped each other out. I've really just been going through the motions for the past year, and having you in my life has liberated me from the dark. I savor being around you, and I'm quite pleased that you are living in the house. You belong here, and I just know there are good times ahead. It feels right...you know? Oh, and by the way"—she added with a twinkle in her eye—"you are hosting Thanksgiving this year. We're going to fill up that fancy table of yours in three weeks, so have it ready." With that, she turned, giggled, and was out the door, leaving Cate gaping.

Cate had so enjoyed her day with Hannah. They possessed similar compatible personalities, and Hannah was always in good humor. Had she not moved to Middleton, they would never have met. It was like Hannah had said; it felt right. She tidied up the kitchen, washed the coffee mugs, headed upstairs, took a hot shower, and crawled into her big comfy bed. She tried to read for a while, but her mind kept turning to the events of the past two months. So much had happened since she arrived here, and even though she still missed David every day, she was content. She closed her eyes and drifted off to sleep, with the lamp still on and her book by her side.

Cate awoke to the sun streaming through her window. She hopped out of bed, stretched herself out, and ran into the bathroom. She peed and washed her hands. Looking into the mirror, she studied her reflection for a minute. That awful haunted look she had worn for the past year had disappeared. She was, after all, only twenty-eight, and she was glad that she looked more like herself these days. She scrubbed her face, brushed her teeth, and put her long hair up in a ponytail. She walked back into the bedroom and looked out the window. It was going to be another glorious fall day. She felt she should take advantage of each and every one before winter blew in—just thinking of it made her cold. She threw on some old yoga pants and a long-sleeved tee, slid her feet into her running shoes, and headed down the stairs. She wanted to get a good start on the dining room set today, so she needed to go to the hardware store a few blocks away for some supplies.

She put coffee on and sat down on a stool to make a list. Two or three grits of sand paper, steel wool, brushes, tack cloth, rags, stain, polyurethane, wood putty and a knife, a plastic tarp, and some paint for the chairs. She needed to dig out the orbital sander from the toolbox in the garage and find a good bucket and sponge for washing the furniture from the pantry.

She poured a cup of coffee, grabbed a banana, and reread her list. She remembered past projects when she had not planned well enough and became annoyed when she realized she had forgotten something and had to run back to the store just when she was getting into the swing of things. It took the wind out of her sails and slowed the whole process down to a crawl. She finished her banana, tossed the peel in the trash, put her mug in the sink, and went into the pantry to find a bucket and sponge and checked it off the list. She rumbled around in the garage, looking for her toolbox, and finally found it in the corner by her gardening tools. She extracted the sander and an extension cord, laid them on the table, and placed the toolbox on a shelf where she should have stored it in the first place.

She grabbed her jacket from one of the hooks, closed and locked the door, and walked across the driveway and down the sidewalk. Ace was only three blocks away. She strolled down the street, taking in the houses and yards as she passed them. It was a pleasant morning, but she could feel a chill in the air and was glad she had put on her jacket. Still, the sun was warm on her face, and there wasn't a cloud in the sky. A tiny jingle bell attached to the door announced her arrival inside the store fifteen minutes later.

A voice from the back called, "I'll be right with you."

Signs over each aisle heralded the items stored within, and Cate had no difficulty locating the items on her list. She was perusing the paint aisle, trying to select the perfect shade of blue for her chairs, when she was startled by a voice behind her apologizing. "I'm sorry for the wait. What can I help you with?"

Cate turned and looked into a pair of eyes as blue as Hannah's. He was probably around fifty, and he stood about six feet tall. His demeanor was kind and helpful. Cate looked at his nametag, Steven.

"Yes," she said. "Can you match this?" She took a swatch out of her pocket and handed it to him.

"I can match anything these days. We have all this fancy technology to help us do just that." He laughed and took the swatch from Cate. "What are you working on?"

"Oh! Um…I'm painting a set of dining room chairs. How much do you think it should take? I have eight chairs."

"Well, I think a couple of quarts should do it, but I'd recommend priming them with a gray primer first. That color is pretty dark, and the primer will hold the paint."

Cate thanked Steven for his expertise, paid for her supplies, and exited the store. There were two fairly heavy bags to carry back, but it was manageable. Cate just imagined she was at the gym working her arms. She had gotten everything on her list and didn't even have to get into her car.

Weren't neighborhoods great? she thought.

She was back at her house in no time at all. She put down her bags and opened up the garage. She had decided she would work from here. A tarp would protect the driveway, and the garage was big enough to accommodate her project. She got to work immediately. Filling her bucket with soap and water, she planned to clean all the pieces first. By the time she finished washing the last chair, the table was already dry enough for sanding. She started with the 100-grit sandpaper. Some people found sanding an odious task, but Cate had always taken pleasure in busy work. She sanded and hummed, hummed and sanded and, at last, stood back to assess her handiwork. She then took out the wood putty and knife and filled in a few spots and scars. After letting that dry for a while, she sanded again. Next, she took a tack cloth and wiped everything down. Then she started over again, this time with the 150 grit. She sanded and cleaned the table four times before she was satisfied with the results. She put away all of the supplies she no longer needed to clear her work space, then she laid down a tarp on the garage floor and maneuvered the table on top of it. It was a large table, and she had to do this with, first, one side, then the other. She opened the stain. The table was a beautiful walnut under all the disgusting crud she had removed. She liked dark wood, so she planned to put several coats of stain on the table top. She carefully painted the stain on, staying with the natural grain of the wood, then rubbed it off again with a rag. It would have to dry before putting on another coat, and her stomach was growling. Just then, something caught her attention at the corner of her eye. She glanced up toward the garage door to find a small girl standing there watching her work.

CHAPTER 4

The Tiny Visitor

The child could not have been more than six. She was very inappropriately dressed considering the chill in the air. She wore little pink shorts and a green tank top. Her tiny little feet were shod in white sandals, with metal rings on the top of each foot. Her long brown hair was caught up in an orange rubber band, but it appeared that her hair hadn't been brushed in a week. She had huge brown eyes, but they held an eerie adult-like expression.

"What are you doing?" she asked matter-of-factly.

At first, Cate was confused. She looked around to see who this child might belong to, but there was no one. She stepped a little farther toward the door and looked both ways up and down the street. There was still no one in sight. At last, Cate found her voice.

"Hi, there!" she said to the child. "I'm working on a table for my dining room."

"Why?" questioned the tiny ragamuffin from the door.

"Because I like to fix old things up and make them new again. Where is your mother?" answered Cate.

"I don't know," stated the child. "Is it hard?"

Cate was trying to decide what to do. She couldn't let this child wander around half-clothed. My goodness! Where was her mother? Had she wandered off? Was she lost? Were people out looking for her? They must be worried out of their minds! Where had she come from? *Oh my*, Cate thought to herself, *I'm so out of my element here!*

"My name is Cate," she whispered as calmly as she could manage. "What is your name, sweetie? Where do you live?" The child must be cold; it was only about 45 degrees outside.

"I'm Kendall…Mama is sleeping. I've been walking and walking…You look nice," she commented as she eyed Cate up and down.

Cate felt the air rush from her lungs. She couldn't wrap her brain around why this child was here and alone. She was at a loss for what to do, so decided first things first—take care of the obvious, then move on to the next thing, one step at a time. The last thing she wanted was to spook this little girl and have her run off to heaven only knows where.

"Well, nice to meet you, Kendall! I have been working on this table all morning, and I'm getting really hungry. Could you eat something?"

Kendall looked up at Cate and smiled. "I think so," she said.

Cate closed the garage door, leaving everything just where it lay. She could deal with all this later. She then headed to the front door. All the while, a million thoughts were racing through her head. She showed Kendall in to the kitchen and helped her to navigate the stool. Kendall was looking all around her, taking everything in.

"Are you cold?" Cate inquired.

"A little. This is pretty," she said, still looking all around her.

Cate made her promise to stay on the stool while she ran upstairs to look for something warmer to put on the child. She searched through her drawers and settled on a sweater that had shrunk in the wash and a pair of socks. She practically ran back downstairs, afraid that Kendall would fall off the stool or harm herself in some other way that Cate couldn't even anticipate right now. She found Kendall still on the stool, looking at everything, taking it all in. She put the sweater over her head, rolled up the sleeves, and tucked her feet into the socks, leaving the little sandals on the floor. The sweater hung to the child's feet, but at least, it would be warm, and it was the best she could do for now. She turned to the fridge and asked Kendall if she would like a ham sandwich and an orange. She was still poking around in the fridge when Kendall answered yes. Cate slathered some mayonnaise on a slice of bread and placed two slices of ham and some lettuce atop, finishing it off with another slice of bread. She then cut it in half, positioning half on one plate, half on another. She chose two oranges from the fruit bowl on the island. Next, she poured out two glasses of milk. She placed a plate and glass in front of Kendall, took a dampened cloth and wiped the child's face and hands, sat on the stool next to the little girl, and began to watch her as she bit into her ham sandwich. She must have been hungry because she made quick work of the first half of the sandwich. Cate watched as she held the orange to her mouth and tried to bite into it.

She took the orange from her and started to peel it as she spoke. "The outside of this orange is a little bitter, so let me peel it for you." She then broke it into sections and put the sections on her plate. "It will be easier to eat this way. Have you had an orange before?" she asked quietly.

"No, pizza and, sometimes, potato chips," she answered. She placed the first section in her mouth, and her eyes lit up with wonder. She gave Cate a huge smile and declared, "I like oranges. Thank you!"

When Kendall had finished eating, Cate helped her down from the stool, took her over to the sink, and washed her hands and face.

"Are you warmer now?" Cate asked.

Kendall shook her head and went to sit on one of the oversized club chairs in the living room. While cleaning up in the kitchen, Cate glanced over to see that Kendall had curled up and fallen asleep. She gently placed a blanket over her, walked over to the phone, dialed Hannah's number, and waited impatiently for her to answer.

When she heard Hannah's cheery hello, she implored, "I need you to come over, right now if you can manage it."

"I'll be there in ten," she stated emphatically. She didn't ask any questions. She hung up the phone and headed out the door toward Cate's immediately.

Cate met her at the door, poured out her story of how she'd found Kendall, everything she had said, and then pointed her out sleeping in the chair. Cate was a bit frantic.

"Do you recognize her? Could she belong to one of your customers? Should I call the police?" she asked in quick succession.

"Calm down," Hannah said. "You have taken care of her immediate needs. She's been fed, she is warm, and she is safe. I don't recognize her. Next, we need to find out if someone is searching for her, so yes, I think calling the police station is in order. Put some coffee on, I think you're going to need some, and so am I."

While Cate was busy making coffee, Hannah dialed the police station.

"Hello, Frank? This is Hannah Miles calling...Yes, it's very good to hear your voice too. Frank, we have a bit of a situation here. I'm over at Cate's. You know, she purchased the Bristol Street house from us? Yes, well, to get right to the point, have any missing children been reported? Oh, I see? Do you think you could come over here? We'll tell you all about it...Yes, okay, we'll watch for you. Thank you, Frank."

Cate handed her a mug and poured her some coffee, then poured a mug for herself. They sat side by side sipping coffee, watching the child sleep, neither speaking a word, when in what seemed like an eternity, they heard a soft knock on the door. Cate started. Hannah rose from the stool and went to answer the door.

"Frank, Hello," Hannah warmly greeted their visitor. "I can't thank you enough for coming over." She repeated what she knew of the situation and then turned to Cate, who still appeared shell-shocked.

"Hello, Cate. I'm Officer Frank Menetta. Please call me Frank. Everyone does." He walked over to the chair that held the child and looked down at her sleeping form. Shaking his head, he said, as if to himself, "I don't think I've seen this little one before. Tell me everything she said to you...try to remember all the details you can." Cate related the events in the order they unfolded. "Did she give you her name?" asked Frank.

"Well, yes...Kendall. I never thought to ask her last name," she fretted.

"You've handled an unusual situation very intelligently," said Frank. "This kind of thing doesn't happen every day. It's certainly not something you can prepare for. I'm so glad it was you she came to!" He searched Cate's face. "Are you doing okay? To tell you the truth, you still look rattled. Should I be worried about you as well?"

Cate smiled. "No, I'm just fine. Thank you so much for coming to us. I just keep thinking her people must be going out of their minds with worry. So…what happens now?" She probed inquiringly.

Hannah offered him some coffee, which he gladly accepted. "Do you take anything in it?" she asked.

"No, thank you. Black is fine." he answered. "Do you mind if I use your phone? I should get in touch with Child Welfare and check to see if we have gotten any inquiries about her yet. I could drive her over to the station, but she looks so comfortable where she is, and I'd hate to wake her just to take her to another unfamiliar place. It's not child friendly. Maybe the social worker can arrange to collect her here, if you don't mind that arrangement?" Frank looked down at her again. "Well, she's no bigger than a minute. How old do you think she is, five or six? I wonder how far she travelled today."

"She is welcome here as long as necessary," Cate asserted, "I'm happy to do whatever I can to help. If you think it's okay, I'd like to send Hannah to pick up a few things for her."

He nodded, and she turned to Hannah and asked, "Do you mind?"

"Not in the least," she responded.

She drove to the mall to purchase some clothing and personal items. No one was sure how much time would pass before the social worker responded or how much longer still until Kendall could be returned to her family or settled in to a safe alternative. Cate would stay here, watching over her in case she woke and needed something.

Frank was in the kitchen on the phone trying to accumulate all the information he could gather. Cate could understand very little from his one-sided conversation and had decided to tune it out completely. Listening in scared her more than if she couldn't hear anything at all.

Kendall stirred, wiggled around, and fell back to sleep. Cate could only smile down at her. She looked so small and helpless curled up in that huge chair. Someone needed to protect this child.

Hannah arrived back carrying three big bags. Cate opened the door for her and inquired, "What on earth? Did you buy out the shopping center?"

Cate's estimation of Hannah grew a little more every day. Of course, this was the kind of thing she would do. It was just her generous nature. She went into the kitchen and started to empty items from the bag.

"I couldn't help it, Cate," she said stubbornly. "I got the pants and realized she would need underwear. I got the hairbrush and thought she'd need hair bows. When I picked out some shoes, I saw the socks nearby. I just couldn't help myself. She can always take these things with her when we find her mom."

Cate stepped up toward her and gave her a big hug. "You, Hannah Miles, are a treasure, and I'm so glad you're my friend. Now let's see what you've spent your money on!"

Hannah extracted two pairs of pants, two shirts, panties, and socks with little lacy hems out the first bag. Cate pulled out a nightie with a princess on the front, a pair of fleecy pajamas with minions on them, a tiny pair of slippers with pink bows, a toothbrush, hairbrush, and hair barrettes from the second bag.

"What's in the last one, Hannah?" Frank asked, laughing as he reached into the last bag and pulled out a warm jacket and a soft-yellow stuffed bunny. Hannah just shrugged, showing her ear-to-ear dimpled grin.

"Now back to the matter at hand," said Frank. "I've spent the last thirty minutes on the phone, but I haven't made much progress. There's still been no report from Dane County or any of the surrounding counties about a missing child. We may have to bring the media in, get a picture of her out there, and hope someone knows who she is. Social work is supposed to return my call at the station, but so far, nothing from them either. I'm not entirely sure that someone is on call. Right now, we're at a standstill. I should get back, in case someone is trying to reach me. Are you prepared to keep Kendall here overnight if it comes to that extreme?"

A little voice squeaked, "Hi, Cate. Is that your bunny?"

"Well, Kendall, about that bunny, I have a proposition for you. If you'll jump into the bathtub and let me wash your hair, you can put on these cozy pajamas"—she answered, holding up the fleece with minions—"and play with this bunny. You can even name him if you want. Do we have a deal?"

She nodded her head and whispered, "Thank you! Can I really name him?"

Cate turned to Frank and told him that things would be fine here since he needed to go. She assured him that she would be awake for hours in case he was successful in his inquiries. She wrote her number down on a pad by the phone and handed it to him, asked Hannah to show him out, and then she turned her attention back to Kendall.

"Of course, you can name him," she promised.

Cate grabbed the PJs, toothbrush, and hairbrush; took Kendall by the hand; and together, they climbed up the stairs to the bathroom. She adjusted the water temperature so that it was warm enough and allowed the tub to fill while she removed the orange rubber band from her dirty tangled hair. She squeezed some toothpaste onto her new tooth brush and explained what it was for because the girl seemed confused by it. She picked Kendall up and helped her down into the tub. As it filled, she soaped a bath cloth, scrubbed her face and back, then handed her the cloth and directed her to "wash up." Next, she shampooed her hair, careful to keep the shampoo from her eyes, and liberally applied conditioner, rinsed everything off, and helped her from the tub. She removed the stopper to drain the tub, assisted in donning the PJs, and gingerly began brushing the tangles from her hair. Kendall was so enthralled with the softness of the pajamas that she took the hair brushing in stride even though there were some killer knots. While brushing out her hair, Cate gently probed for more information.

"Do you know your last name Kendall?" Cate asked delicately.

"My name is Kendall..." she answered.

"Can you tell me where you live?" Cate inquired softly.

"I live in a blue house with Mama," she answered solemnly.

"Could you show me where it is?" asked Cate.

"No, I can't find it," she stated firmly, beginning to cry for the first time all day.

Cate reassured her that everything would be okay and asked if she knew her mother's name, and when Kendall shook her head, Cate got excited until she answered Mama. Cate didn't have the heart to press her further, so with bath time accomplished, she tidied the room and headed down the stairs. Kendall padded down the stairs, following Cate like a puppy.

"Kendall, this is Hannah." She pointed toward Hannah by way of introduction. "She chose those pajamas and this bunny just for you."

"She did? Really...I can keep him?" she asked wondrously, searching Hannah's face for an answer. Hannah smiled down at her and nodded her head.

Hannah squatted down to Kendall's level, looked right into her big brown eyes, and inquired, "Have you thought of a name for him yet?"

Kendall reached up to hug her, patted her white hair softly, and planted a small kiss on her cheek.

"I think I'll call him Bunny," she replied earnestly. Then she turned, walked to the living room, and crawled up into the club chair where she had slept earlier. There, she proceeded to hold a very serious conversation with Bunny. Hannah walked over to the chair and placed the pink slippers on her feet.

"We have to keep your feet warm," she stated matter-of-factly.

Kendall simply beamed up at her and began to describe, in detail, her lovely slippers and pajamas to Bunny.

"I love you, Bunny," she chirped, then yawned and sat quietly, stroking her new toy. In mere moments, she was sound asleep again.

Poor thing, she's had such a long day, Cate thought as she lifted her up and proceeded to ascend the stairs, cradling her tenderly. She worried about the unfamiliar surroundings while positioning her gently on the white bed. She covered her with the soft-yellow bedding and turned on the diminutive lamp on the bedside table in an effort to keep Kendall from being frightened if she woke in the night. Cate's room was right next door. Hopefully, that would be good enough. She turned and bounded down the steps. When she reached the kitchen, she gave Hannah a wild look, poured herself a cup of coffee, and hunkered down on the stool beside her friend. *My goodness! What a day!* The phone rang, and Hannah hopped up to answer it and handed it over to Cate.

Frank said to expect Karen Martin, the social worker, on Monday morning. He explained that there had been no one on call, and she was currently out of town for the weekend. She would have come directly had she been close by. He further explained that if Kendall's family could be located, that situation would be evaluated, and they would determine what was best for the child at that time. No results locating the parents or further identifying Kendall yet. Cate reported the little information she had gotten from the little girl, and Frank asked how she felt about the possibility of a house guest for another night and was assured that, of course, all was fine.

It was nearly nine by this point. Cate told Hannah that she thought she would be up all night between all the coffee she had consumed and the events of the day. They talked together for another hour, trying to imagine what could have happened to lead to this small child wandering all over Middleton alone, and why had no one reported her as missing. She had been with them for almost eight hours. Cate observed that she was a trusting child, well-behaved, and polite. She related her reaction to the toothbrush and her being unfamiliar with the orange to Hannah.

"I wonder what her story is?" she asked Hannah rhetorically. "Something feels peculiar that I can't quite put my finger on."

Hannah rose from the uncomfortable stool, rubbing her back, and said lightheartedly, "Well, you better get on that dining room set and buy yourself a sofa soon if you want my company. I can't perch on that stool for hours at a time!" She gave Cate a hug and promised to return in the morning.

As Cate was still wide awake, she opened the door that adjoined the kitchen to the garage, turned the overhead light on, and approached the table. The first coat took very well, and she couldn't detect the repairs she had made with the wood putty; however, it was still too light. She envisioned a rich deep-mahogany color, so she reopened the stain and proceeded to brush on another coat and again to rub it off and leaving it to dry. She pushed forward to finish the chairs. Thoughts of Kendall raced through her head as she worked. In less than two hours, she had primed and painted all eight chairs. The finish on the table was still tacky, so she turned off the overhead lights and closed the door. She would check on them tomorrow. She was quite tired now and thought she may be able to sleep, and for the last time tonight, she climbed the stairs and turned into the bathroom, where she lost herself in a long luxurious bath. Before going to bed, she peered into the room where Kendall slept. Satisfied that she was fine, Cate wriggled into her own bed and fell immediately to sleep. Hours later, she awakened to find Kendall scrutinizing her.

"Hello, Cate, are you sleeping?"

Cate couldn't help but smile. "Good morning, sweetie. No, I'm awake. Did you sleep well?" she answered as she rolled over and sat on the edge of the bed stretching.

"Yes. Can I go home now?" she asked tentatively. She shook her little head from side to side. "Mama will be mad."

Cate had thought about the idea that Kendall's family would be worried, but she hadn't contemplated that Kendall might be feeling panicked. She explained that Officer Menetta was trying to find her family, but they didn't know where she lived yet. She considered driving around the neighborhoods nearby in case Kendall could recognize something, but she didn't own a booster seat, and she wasn't sure what kind of situation the child might be living in, so she quickly nixed that idea until she could ask Frank's opinion.

"Let's have some breakfast and get dressed. We can plan our day after we eat, okay?" Cate stated convincingly as she gauged Kendall's big brown eyes for a reaction. Reading no fear in them, she took her by the hand, led her down the stairs, and perched her up on a stool. "What do you like for breakfast? Fruit, cereal, or eggs?"

"Pizza!" cried Kendall with a mischievous grin on her face.

"Pizza?" repeated Cate. "For breakfast? I don't even think I have any pizza."

"Don't you like pizza?" breathed Kendall suspiciously. "Everybody likes pizza. Where's Bunny?" she murmured to herself as she searched the room with her eyes.

Cate meandered around the room until she spied Bunny lying on a club chair across the foyer in the living room. She plucked it from the chair and delivered it into Kendall's arms. The girl smiled and petted him. Pouring some coffee into the filter and adding water to the pot, she turned her attention to food and plucked up an apple and an orange from the fruit bowl on the island and then took a container of pineapple from the fridge. Divvying up the chunks between two bowls, she managed an appetizing fruit salad. Next, she warmed up some milk in a little sauce pan on the stove, stirred in a little cocoa and sweetener she had found in the pantry, poured it into a mug small hands could embrace, and topped it off with a couple of marshmallows. Placing the bowl and mug in front of Kendall, she directed her to put Bunny down for a bit and eat her breakfast, and Kendall complied without a complaint. She ate all the fruit and nursed the cocoa.

"It's too hot now," she explained when Cate asked if she wanted something different.

Cate let her choose which outfit to wear, and she picked the blue jeans and the long-sleeved shirt with some flowers on the front. She trotted up to the bathroom to retrieve the hairbrush so Cate could arrange her hair in barrettes. She checked herself out in a mirror in the living room and, to show her approval, ran up to Cate and hugged her.

She asked if she could watch TV, and Cate acquiesced. "For an hour, okay?"

Kendall nodded her head and scampered back to the living room, turning on the TV, and searching for a channel she approved of. Cate could now hear Sesame Street in the background.

Hannah arrived and asked how the night had gone. Cate told her that everything went smoothly but shared that Kendall had asked to go home this morning.

"I hope that Frank has some news for us soon," she replied. "Good news is I got the chairs painted, and I think the table just needs polyurethane to be complete. I'll check in a few minutes. Could I talk you into helping me bring them inside? I was up until around one this morning since I was wound so tight. Slept like a baby when I finally turned in though."

Just then, the phone rang. Cate grabbed the receiver, conversed for a few minutes, and hung up again.

"Frank's on his way over," she spoke nervously. "It seems he has some news for us."

Frank arrived fifteen minutes later, and since Kendall was engrossed in the television, Cate allowed her to keep watching. It served as a diversion for Kendall so the adults could talk privately.

"Well, it was nearly an impossible task," Frank began. "The only physical information we had was the blue house, and we couldn't even be sure of that since it came from a five-year-old, but we got lucky. Early this morning, we received a call about something suspicious at an address over on Columbus Drive. One of the neighbors noticed that a door was open. When they called out, no one answered, so they called us. We sent a patrol car over to investigate and found Kendall's mother at the bottom of the steps leading into the basement. Now, she's going to be okay, but she suffered some pretty bad breaks and is now hospitalized. I'm afraid she's going to be out of commission for several weeks. The last thing she could recall was Kendall lying on the floor beside her. Apparently, she was doing the laundry yesterday morning and took a tumble while carrying her clothes downstairs. She reported that she was in and out of consciousness. She was in a lot of pain but was frantic about Kendall. She said she had been calling for help, but nobody heard her. The poor thing had been lying down there for nearly twenty-four hours when we found her. She also has pneumonia now in addition to a broken tibia and two breaks in her fibula. We assured her that Kendall is being cared for right now and that she should get some rest. She phoned her mother who is semi-retired and lives in Cedar Rapids, and she is on the way here...should be arriving in two to three more hours. There appears to be no foul play. We think while Jenny—that's Kendall's mom—was unconscious, Kendall dressed herself and left the house. Maybe, at first, she was looking for help but, seeing no one, walked too far and simply got lost. An angel must have been on that child's shoulder yesterday. Columbus Drive is three miles from here, and she had to have walked across at least two busy streets. Jenny has a lot to be thankful for today, but she's a single mom, and she'll have a long road ahead. Looks like you and Hannah are heroines. Someone will come to collect Kendall after lunch. Is that reasonable? We really appreciate that you stepped up because, honestly, I'm not sure where she would have ended up. This whole situation has been tragic, but it has a happy ending not many of my cases do."

He said his goodbyes, declared it was a pleasure to have met Cate, tipped his officer's cap at Hannah, waved goodbye to Kendall, and was out the door.

Kendall turned the TV off. "Did he find my house?" she asked nervously and searched Cate's face for answers. "Mama will be mad."

Cate picked her up and carried her into the kitchen, plopping her down on a stool.

"Kendall," she began, "Officer Menetta found your house and found your mother. Your mother fell and broke her leg, but the doctors at the hospital are fixing that up for her. She isn't mad at you. She is only worried about you. Officer Menetta made sure that she knows where you are and that you are okay here with me and Hannah. Your grandmother is coming to get you this afternoon to take you home, so I don't want you to worry anymore. Everything is going to be okay."

Kendall didn't say anything, but big tears began to fall silently down her face. She reached to give Cate a big hug, then turned to Hannah and smiled through her tears. Cate and Hannah shared a smile of relief over her head.

"We are going to have a very busy day!" announced Hannah emphatically. "Why don't we help Cate finish the dining room and then we can bake some cookies for your mother. I am an excellent baker!" She grinned. "Would you like that?"

Kendall nodded her head excitedly and clapped her hands together.

Working as a team, they managed to get all of the pieces from the garage into the dining room. Hannah realized the blue on the chairs really worked in the space and complemented the pops of blue in the Fiesta ware atop the open shelving in the kitchen. Cate had decided that it would be easier to carry everything inside and then she could finish the table top at her leisure. It only needed a few coats of poly to make it shine. Hannah looked around the space and had to admit that Cate knew how to design a room. It was inviting and would be very serviceable. Cate would be able to accommodate ten people easily between the dining room and the island. All for the low, low price of forty dollars. Hannah giggled to herself, remembering her doubt at the estate sale.

With Kendall's help, Hannah was examining the ingredients in the pantry. "We have everything we need to make chocolate chip, peanut butter, or my personal favorite, oatmeal raisin. What do you think?" she asked, looking down into Kendall's big brown eyes.

"Chocolate chip!" Kendall blurted, giggling up at Hannah.

She had been really quite animated since learning that her mother was okay, and it was a joy to watch. They plucked items from the shelves and carried them into the kitchen, placing them on the island. Hannah preheated the oven, located some measuring cups, a bowl, a big wooden spoon, and a couple of cookie sheets. She picked up a stool and put it down on the kitchen side of the island so Kendall could perch on it to help since the island was too high for her. They began mixing ingredients, chattering and laughing together, and soon, Kendall's face was covered in flour. She was having the time of her life.

As she busied herself in the dining room, applying the first coat of poly, Cate found herself smiling at the exchange going on in the kitchen. *A miniature baker in the making*, she thought cheerfully and offered up a prayer of thanks for the way this situation had transpired. In spite of how stressful and tiring the last twenty-four hours had been, she discovered that she felt invigorated and very much alive. She'd spent the past year buried under anger outrage, and grief. It was high time she rejoined the human race. David would certainly not want her to wallow in misery for the rest of her life. In just one short month, she had finally come full circle, and she intended to make the most of her reprieve. She glanced into the kitchen, watching Hannah place the cookie sheets into the oven. She had no doubt that she would still encounter moments of depression, probably even days, but in this moment, she felt only gratitude and peace.

"If you girls are finished making a big mess in my kitchen, maybe we can think about lunch. What shall it be?" she called.

"Pizza," shouted Kendall instantaneously.

"Well, Hannah," Cate responded, "I think she is suffering from withdrawal. Shall we order pizza?"

"You bet," answered Hannah enthusiastically. "I'll take these cookies out to cool while the two of you decide what you want on it." She removed both pans from the oven, setting them aside to cool, and replaced them with two more. Then, heading toward the phone she inquired "What will it be?" as she dialed from memory.

"Pepperoni," called Cate.

"Cheese," called Kendall, simultaneously laughing.

"Right! One large half pepperoni, half double cheese pizza coming right up." And she placed her order. She stepped into the pantry and returned with paper plates and napkins. "I saw these earlier," she said as she placed them on the island. Then she turned, took the other two pans from the oven, put them aside, and turned the knob to off. "These do smell divine. Kendall and I made some for her mother and some for Officer Menetta, didn't we, sweetheart? I'll bet we have enough so that we can each have one for dessert though," she grinned. She commenced cleaning off the island and put the dishes in the sink for later. "I sure will be glad when we can actually spread out at the table. You have done a great job with it." She complimented Cate. "Are you going to put another coat on it?"

"Yes, two more coats, I think, but it should dry overnight between coats." Turning in response to a knock at the door, she called, "Pizza!"

They finished their pizza, with Kendall and Hannah atop the two stools, and Cate pulled up one of the blue chairs to the island. She was sitting so low that her shoulders were even with the surface. Kendall found this very funny indeed and giggled right through her meal. Hannah packaged the cookies up into two tidy bundles and placed them on the island. She had managed to make them look like presents tied up with some multicolored ribbons she had found who knows where and plastic wrap. Then she returned to the sink to wash up the dishes.

Cate asked Kendall to check her bathroom and bedroom to make sure all her things were accounted for, while she folded her clothes and gathered all of the personal belongings that Hannah had purchased and packed them all neatly into a little fabric carryall with daisies on the side. She placed the bag by the door in the foyer.

They all ambled into the living room to wait. Kendall sprawled on the floor, embracing Bunny, while Cate tuned the TV to PBS KIDS again for her. She and Hannah sat across from one another in the club chairs, discreetly discussing the happenings of the weekend. Cate was unsuccessfully trying to describe her feelings of optimism to Hannah when the doorbell rang, ending the conversation before it had really begun. Cate jumped up to answer the door. Frank stood at the door with a middle-aged woman attired in a navy-blue jogging suit. Cate stepped aside to allow them to enter.

"Cate, Hannah, this is Margie Campion, Kendall's grand-mother," he said. Kendall looked around, got up, and ran into her grandmother's arms.

Cate shook her hand. "It's a pleasure to meet you," she expressed as she offered her the club chair opposite Hannah. Hannah half rose and nodded, then stuck out her hand in greeting.

"I'm so sorry for the lack of seating," Cate apologized. "I'm new to the area, and the house isn't quite finished yet. Frank, would you be so kind as to grab one of those chairs from the dining room for yourself. Can I offer either of you something to drink? How about some coffee, a soft drink, or water, perhaps?

"Nothing for me," Margie answered sincerely. "And please, don't apologize. I am so indebted to you for taking such good care of Kendall. Officer Menetta has filled me in on all you have done for her, and I'm so grateful to you both. I can't even imagine what would have happened if you had not found my granddaughter." She took a seat and Kendall popped up on her lap and smothered her with kisses.

"It was a pleasure for us, Mrs. Campion, and Kendall found us, not the other way around. She is a delightful child, and we are all very pleased that we could help. How is your daughter?" she inquired.

"Thank you for asking. She is making strides," informed Mrs. Campion. "She will probably remain hospitalized for another week

45

or so, but she'll come around. I'm going to take Kendall to see her for a little while when we leave here. I think she'll rest more easily if she can see for herself that her daughter is in one piece, and no doubt, Kendall also needs to see her mother."

"I'll have a cup of coffee if you have some made," Frank said. "Please don't go to any trouble though. We can't stay very long. Margie wants to get back to the hospital."

"Kendall, sweetie, don't you have something for Officer Menetta?" asked Hannah.

She nodded her head happily and scampered off into the kitchen to fetch her present. She hurried back and placed one bag into Frank's hand. "This one is for you"—and holding up the other—"and this one is for Mama," and placed it in the bag by the door. She smiled over at Frank. "Hannah helped me make these today," she told him.

Cate brought a cup of coffee in and handed it to Frank.

"You made these cookies for me? That is pretty special, Kendall! Thank you so much! I'm going to eat one right now," he said as he gracefully unwrapped the packaging and stuffed an entire cookie into his mouth. He quickly gobbled it down, making Kendall squeal with delight. "That was the best cookie I ever ate. I just might have to have another." When he looked over at Kendall, she was beaming.

They rose to leave, and Kendall blew kisses and gave hugs all around.

"Don't forget your bag and Bunny over by the door. I put my phone number in the bag, just in case you want to let me know how you're doing. I'm sure your grandmother or your mother will help you dial. Take care, sweetie!" she called from the door.

Frank waved goodbye, and they were off. Hannah and Cate took up residence in the club chairs again. Cate looked around the room and sighed.

"Well, one thing's for sure. Tomorrow, I'm going to go buy a sofa," she declared and smirked at Hannah to make her laugh.

CHAPTER 5

A Family Home

"I'm serious Cate!" Hannah looked her friend in the eye. "How are you doing? This was a lot to take on, and I know you were getting attached to that girl."

"That is what I was trying to explain earlier. I'm fine," she said as she returned her friend's stare. "I'm better than fine. I feel like we have done something really important here, Hannah. I've stopped thinking about my own problems and concentrated on someone else's, and I feel"—she paused, searching for the words—"gratified, satisfied…elated. How do you feel about all this?"

"Do you really want my opinion?" she asked thoughtfully as she sat more upright in her chair, searching Cate's face. Seeing her friend nod, she continued on. "I am a firm believer that everything happens for a reason. I believe we were meant to come into each other's lives. I believe that you were meant to live in this house, and I imagine that there is much more to come that we can't even fathom right now. Is that deep enough for you?"

Cate looked at her friend and spoke admiringly, "Exactly!"

Hannah broke into Cate's thoughts and said, "Enough seriousness for one day! It's still early. Let's go buy you a sofa so you can invite more than one person to sit down at a time for crying out loud." They donned their jackets and decided to take Hannah's Subaru in to Madison since it was blocking the drive.

As they strolled into the store, Cate saw almost immediately just what she was looking for. It was a large brown sectional that would easily seat six or even seven. It boasted nailhead trim that would tie in with the club chairs. The fabric was high-thread-count chenille and luxurious to the touch. They wandered around the store, searching for a salesperson, when she also spied a bunk bed that she was drawn to.

"We need to find someone to help us with the order before I find something else I can't resist." Cate laughed.

The sale was finalized; arrangements were made to have everything delivered the following day. They decided to have dinner out and settled on a little café back in Middleton on Hubbard Street. Cate ordered the white chicken chili, and Hannah chose the Italian eggplant panini, which she later described as a little taste of heaven and allowed Cate to taste. They finished the meal, divided the check, and Hannah dropped Cate off in front of her house.

Hannah was opening the bakery tomorrow, but Cate wasn't scheduled until Wednesday and Thursday this week, so she still had a couple of days to herself. She checked the table once she entered the house and decided it was dry enough to apply another coat of polyurethane. Brushing the viscous golden liquid on the tabletop for the second time, she wondered if two coats might end up being enough. Morning would tell; she could decide then.

She moved some of the packed boxes, most of which held books that would be placed on the bookshelves flanking the fireplace in the living room in, order to accommodate the arrival of the sofa tomorrow and tore down several dozen of the empties that had ended here from unpacking in other parts of the house and took them out into the garage to place in the recycle bin. The room already looked more spacious. She arranged the club chairs on the left by the window, with a table between, and placed a lamp with a cream-colored linen shade atop the table. Standing back and looking critically at the vignette, she decided she approved the look. The sofa would sit against the wall on the right so that one could view the television or the fireplace from that position. She didn't approve trifles cluttering up her space so only displayed items with a purpose like her books and her dishes. She was restless, so she began opening boxes and relocating books to shelves and, within an hour, had completed that chore and had six more boxes broken down for recycling, which she trotted out to the garage. Glancing at the clock, she noticed that the time was nearly eleven, and she had succumbed to exhaustion. It was time for a shower and bed.

She awakened with the sun streaming on her face. Squinting to see her clock, she saw it was eight fifteen. Goodness! She must have been tired last night. Sleeping nine hours away was unheard of for her. Scrambling out of bed, she went into the bathroom to wash her face and brush her teeth. Tidying up the bathroom and making her bed were first on her agenda, then as she walked from the bathroom, she stopped for a moment to gaze into the yellow bedroom and decided to strip the linens from the bed to be washed. She sat down on the bed for a moment, dirty linens in her arms, and recalled the image of Kendall sleeping here and smiled. She was lost, deep in thought, when the phone's ringing jerked her back to reality. Dropping the laundry in front of the laundry room door, she rushed into her bedroom to answer the phone.

"Hello, McCarthy residence, Cate speaking," she answered.

"Hello, Mrs. McCarthy, my name is Martin, Karen Martin. You don't know me, but I've been told a lot about you, and I wonder if you would have some time in your schedule to talk with me. I could come to you. I work for the Department of Human Services, and I got your name from Officer Frank Menetta. I hope it's not too early to call."

"Um, no. I've been up for a little while. You are aware that Kendall is back with her family?"

"Yes, I am. Mrs. McCarthy, is today a good day for you?" she answered.

"I'm expecting a delivery today, so I plan to stay in. You're welcome to come by if you like. Do you have my address? Yes, it's 222 Bristol Street, white house, blue shutters. Okay, I look forward to meeting you."

She walked back to the laundry room and began loading the washer and thought that was a curious conversation. I wonder what she wants to talk about. She padded back to her room and dressed in jeans and a T-shirt, wriggled into her shoes and bounced down the stairs to assess the dining room table. Placing her hand gingerly over the surface, she concluded that two coats was enough. She took a tack cloth and polished the whole tabletop. She stood back and marveled at how well it turned out. It looked custom-made for this space. She shook her head as she reflected—forty bucks.

Bringing the chair that Frank had used back from the living room and settling it once again in its place, her thoughts turned to the all-important cup of coffee, so she sauntered toward the kitchen to brew a pot. Mentally, she ticked items off her list as she accomplished them throughout the day—laundry, check; rolling the trash and recycling out to the curb for pickup, check; mopping floors, check. It was nearly ten-thirty. Since she'd only had coffee and toast for breakfast, she was anticipating lunch. She added butter to a Dutch oven, prepared a mirepoix, and gently stirred until they became translucent, then lowered the heat. She rifled through the refrigerator and located some deboned rotisserie chicken, a couple of zucchini, and a jar of her homemade vegetable stock. She added the chicken and the stock and went to work chopping the zucchini and poured them into the mix. She turned the burner to simmer and picked up the mess she'd just made. She recalled a jar of wild rice stored in the pantry, retrieved it, and added a cup to the pot simmering away on the stove. She phoned Hannah and invited her to come over for soup when she had finished at the bakery and asked her to bring some crusty bread. She was wiping down the counter when she heard the knock and traipsed over to open the door.

The delivery guys asked for her signature on the delivery slip and proceeded to offload her furniture and haul it into the house.

"The sofa goes right here against this wall." She pointed. "And the bunks go upstairs, second room on the right. Do you set them up?" she inquired and was assured that they would set everything up and remove all the packing materials. She was admiring the sectional when another knock on the door captured her attention.

"Hello, Mrs. McCarthy. I'm Karen Martin. Have I interrupted something?" said the smiling petite thirty-something businesswoman standing on her porch with her hand outstretched. Cate returned her smile, shook her hand, and opened the door wide to allow her to enter.

"Not at all," she responded. "I'm having some furniture delivered, but I'm sure they're almost finished. Please, have a seat. You can initiate the sectional. It's just arrived. May I offer you something to drink?"

"No, thank you," she answered, looking around the room. "You have a beautiful home, and something smells heavenly in here."

"Thank you. I'm making chicken soup. This house has been a lot of work, but I was lucky to find it, and it's almost complete now. I'll have to share the story with you one day. I could give you a little tour when the delivery people go if you'd like.

"I'd like that very much." Karen rubbed the fabric of the sectional and asserted, "I think you have a winner here. This is so comfortable and roomy."

The guys came down the stairs. Cate offered them coffee or water, but they declined, thanked her for the business, and were on their way. "Please call if there are any problems at all," the tall one said as he waved and strolled out the door.

Cate turned her attention back to Karen. "Would you like that tour now?" She led Karen into the dining room, through to the kitchen, allowed her to peek into the pantry, showed her past the main level bathroom and up the stairs to view the bedrooms. Karen peered into the yellow bedroom and then into the room that now housed the bunk beds that had just arrived. One room stood completely empty, and the last must have belonged to Cate. She noted the two full baths on this floor. The place was charming. *It wasn't just a house; it was a home*, she thought.

They descended the stairs, at which point, Karen asked, "Can I take you up on that coffee now? You must be wondering why I've come."

Cate nodded, directed her to the dining room to sit. She put some prepackaged cookies on a little plate and brought two mugs of coffee and placed them on the table.

"Do you take anything in your coffee?" she asked. Karen shook her head. She joined Karen at the table, sat, and sipped her coffee silently for a few moments. "I have to admit. I have been curious."

The door opened, and Hannah called out, "Hi, Cate, I'm here."

"We're in the dining room," called Cate.

She made the introductions. She explained that Hannah was her closest friend and encouraged Karen to feel free to share whatever was on her mind. She got another mug of coffee for Hannah and returned to the table. Hannah was astounded by how well the table had turned out.

"You were right about this table," she announced, "as usual."

Karen looked across the table and intimated, "You have a lovely home here, Cate. I appreciate you taking the time to show me around. However, I can't help but wonder why you chose such a large home when you live alone or why, for that matter, do you have bunk beds upstairs. The last thing I want to do is to pry or offend. Your business is just that, your business. I've worked with Frank Menetta for several years. He related the situation with Kendall to me in detail. He couldn't crow enough about the two of you. I was amazed by what you and Hannah did. Not everyone would have taken in a strange child, no matter the circumstances. Kendall could have been traumatized or even harmed, but she is safely ensconced back in the arms of her family and is no worse off than she was before this happened. That is cause for celebration, and I salute you both.

"Allow me to share some ugly facts with you. There are over three million reports of abuse in this country every year involving greater than six million minor children. There are between four and seven fatalities of children every day, and it is estimated that 50 percent or better are not even reported. Child abuse spans every socio-economic level. It crosses every ethnic and cultural line, and the costs of abuse in the US alone are in the billions. We have a huge problem, and I believe you can help. Shall I continue, or do you want to throw me out on my ear?" she said guardedly.

"Well," Cate responded warily, "that is certainly a lot to take in. I'm going to need a little time to digest this information. Do you have somewhere you need to be? I have soup on the stove if you'd like to share a bowl with us and fill us in on exactly what it is that you are proposing."

"I'd be pleased to join you. I am absolutely famished, and the aroma of your soup is driving me to distraction," she remarked. "May I use your restroom?"

Cate set the table with three colossal stoneware bowls and filled three glasses with ice water. She poured the soup into a blue Fiesta ware tureen, sprinkled some parsley on the top, and set it on the table on a red fabric table protector. She planted a large silicon ladle beside the soup dish. While Hannah stood by the island slicing bread on a heavy wooden cutting board, Cate grabbed the butter from the fridge, three napkins and some spoons from a drawer, and returned to the table. Hannah arrived carrying the whole cutting board, sat it down by the soup tureen, and slid herself into a chair.

"The soup smells delectable, Cate. Can we dig in? I haven't eaten since six," Hannah moaned.

Cate laughed at her friend. "Have at it," she said. They served themselves from the tureen, passed the bread and butter around the table. and kept the conversation to small talk while they ate. "This bread is scrumptious," raved Cate.

"Thanks, pal," shot Hannah. "So is this soup! I could drink it down with a funnel!" She finished her bowl, wiped her mouth with her napkin, pushed her bowl aside and, looking at Karen, said, "All joking aside, tell us what's on your mind."

Karen pushed her dishes away, crossed her arms on top of the table, and spoke intently. "There are many options to choose from, but because of what I have observed here, I think the thing for you is Emergency Foster Care. We are in desperate need.

"This is a family home, a place large enough to accommodate more than one child at a time. You have demonstrated your ability to handle a delicate situation and remain unruffled. You are intelligent and capable. Emergency Foster Care is exactly what the name implies—somewhere we can place children with very little notice when they are endangered and in crisis. Unlike regular foster care, which is also open to you, Emergency Foster Care is short term. Usually, less than thirty days, until we can place them in a more permanent situation, hopefully, with other family members. Often, it is a sibling situation where all the children must be removed for their own safety. You must be available twenty-four seven when children are in your care, so I'm hoping that between the two of you, that won't be a problem. We offer specialized training and a stipend to cover some expenses. You have to furnish household items, transportation, and the like on your own. You will have support from my office and Frank's department. We always try to have a social worker on call, but there are times when you'll have to deal with difficulties on your own.

"It will be heartbreaking, and it will be rewarding. You will see things you should never have to see and will never forget. It will cost you very dearly emotionally, but trust me when I say it will be the most important work you'll ever do. Not everyone can do it, but I believe you can. I don't want an answer today. I'll leave you with some information to read and my number. Take your time and consider it very carefully. My number is on the pamphlet on the top of the packet. It has been a pleasure to meet you both. I'll let myself out, and I'll await your call."

As soon as Karen had closed the door behind her, Hannah let out a whistle and started to pick up the dishes from the table and carried them to the sink.

"Sorry, Cate, this is big, and by big, I mean huge! What are you thinking? Oh, for crying out loud! I already know what you're thinking. You want to take this on, don't you?"

Cate, searching for a storage container for the leftover soup, was frustratingly silent. When she finally found one of the proper size, she walked back over to the table, poured the soup into the container, closed the lid, and sat down again.

"I don't think I can function yet," she murmured under her breath.

Hannah left the dishes soaking in the sink and rejoined Cate at the table. Together, they sat in silence for over half an hour.

Cate rose at last, drifted into the kitchen to deposit the soup in the refrigerator. "We need to educate ourselves," she whispered. "We can't possibly make this kind of decision without more information. Where is that packet Karen left for us?" She looked around. She located it on the table in the living room and brought it back to the table, opened it up, and emptied the contents in front of Hannah. Out spilled pages of statistics, lists of support personnel, and even some case files were included, but they were scenarios without mention of any identifying information. Nevertheless, they were heart-wrenching stories. Cate stood, patted Hannah on the back, and said quietly "I think we should sleep on this, but I've got to tell you, Hannah, I'm leaning toward a yes. I don't know how we could refuse."

Hannah looked up and responded, "I agree. This is important, and we are in a position to help. If it's too terrible, we can bow out. But think of the good we can do. Imagine the difference we can make. Why don't you stop in for breakfast in the morning, and we can talk about it further? That will give us time to consider all of our options. I have some errands to run. See you in the morning?" Cate nodded and walked Hannah to the door, waiting as she wound her way down the paver pathway toward her Subaru.

Cate stepped onto the porch and out onto the lawn, waving as Hannah drove away. She turned and examined the exterior of the house. She then reentered and strolled through every room, ending in the bedroom that now housed the brand-new bunk beds. She crawled in and sat on the bottom bunk, crossed her legs, and regarded the space as a child might. It was a sizable room. She could easily fit another bed in here if necessary. She had never raised a child. She had no earthly idea how to go about it. She might screw it up completely. Could she do more harm than good? Would she have the patience required to parent damaged children—and there was no doubt in her mind that would be exactly what she was signing up for. It all came down to one thing. She could offer children in peril a safe haven. She couldn't think of a more noble cause. She was in.

Cate awoke with a start at around five. She had been dreaming that there were a bunch of children banging on her door, but she couldn't get the door to open. They were crying and knocking, calling out for her, but no matter what she did, the door refused to open. Shaking it off, she found herself glad to be awake. *Good grief, must have too much on my mind*, she thought.

She went into the bathroom to wash her face and brush her teeth. She pulled on a tunic-length sweater, leggings, and black boots. She brushed her hair but left it down, falling in ringlets The bakery wouldn't be open for another half hour, and she couldn't wait that long for coffee, besides, Hannah was always so busy first thing when she opened, so she went downstairs to brew a pot. Sitting at the island, sipping from her mug, she tried to make a mental note of things she wanted to accomplish today but simply couldn't prioritize between what she needed to do versus what she imagined she needed to do. She had to work twelve-hour shifts for the next two days so probably wouldn't have time for much other than work on those days. She needed to talk to Hannah before making any far-reaching decisions, so she took a coat from the closet and started down the sidewalk toward the bakery.

Cate bumped into Frank on the sidewalk in front of the bakery. He was also heading in for breakfast, and Cate felt rather surprised to realize that she was pleased to see him.

"Hello, Cate," he said cheerfully. "Good to see you. Are you just arriving? Maybe we can share a table, and you can tell me how you've been doing. I've been a little worried about you."

Cate smiled up at him and nodded. "Of course," she responded. "Hannah and I are making some hefty decisions today, and actually, maybe you could answer a few questions for us?"

"It would be my pleasure, and if I'm not mistaken, I owe you one, so anything for a lady in need" he answered playfully. He held the door for her and placed his hand on the small of her back and led her in to a table near the window. "Can I hang up your coat?" he asked, pointing. "There's a rack over there with hooks." He took her coat and shouted out to Hannah, laughing. "Look what I found outside!"

She came around the counter with two mugs and the coffee pot. "Good morning," she sang. "Here's your coffee. What would you like to go with it?" Cate ordered a croissant and, Frank, pumpkin bread.

"You have to try Hannah's pumpkin bread. It's amazing." Holding up three fingers, he said, "Scout's honor. She spreads cream cheese frosting on the top too. I'll let you have a bite of mine."

"It's been busy this morning, so it might be awhile before I can join you, Cate." And she was off to fetch their order. In no time,

Hannah was scurrying back with their food. She plunked it down on the table, smiled, and kept on going.

Frank eyed Cate and said earnestly, "I hope you aren't upset about me sending Karen around to talk to you yesterday. Have you given any thought to her proposition?"

"I've done nothing but think about it. I even dreamed about it last night," she stated. "I'm not upset. Honestly, I'm flattered that you'd think I can handle this. I believe I've come to a decision, but for this to work, Hannah has to agree. I'll need her help if we commit to this, and I haven't had a chance to talk to her yet. There is still a lot to consider."

He liked the little crease in her brow that appeared when she was involved in serious conversation. Frank tore off a piece of his pumpkin bread and offered it to her to break the tension.

"Seriously, you have to try this!" he exclaimed.

"Umm, that is mighty tasty," she said truthfully. "I guess that's another of Hannah's specialties to add to my list. That list is growing daily." She laughed.

He liked the way she laughed, how her smile lit up her whole face. He noticed her hair was down and didn't think he'd seen it worn down before. It had always been tied up in a ponytail like a young girl's, and he sure was a fan of long hair. Actually, he suddenly realized, so far, there wasn't anything he didn't like about her, and he wasn't at all sure how he felt about that knowledge. He needed to step back and be careful, he thought.

"You said you had some questions I might be able to answer. What's on your mind?" he inquired.

"I have questions for Karen about the logistics of foster care, but I thought you might give me some insight about the commitment. You must know people who do this? What happens when you think you can handle it but find you were just kidding yourself? Above everything else, I'm afraid of making an already intolerable situation worse."

"I do know some people involved in foster care," he pondered. "Not Emergency Foster Care, the long-term version. It's a little different than Emergency Care. Foster care is a commitment of maybe a year or two. With your situation, it would be a few days, not more than thirty days at most, if I remember correctly. I'd be glad to make some calls and see if they would speak to you about their experiences. It's a tricky thing because of privacy issues, but I'll check it out for you. I know there are multiple levels of care and the more difficult a situation, the more training is required. I don't think you'd be thrown into a situation you were entirely unprepared for.

"Imagine that you are the only place these kids have to go—for tonight, for right now. They have been hurt, and they are angry and traumatized. For many of them, this won't be the first time. They find it very difficult to trust anyone. Why should they? Why hold out your hand only to have it slapped? They learn quickly. Sometimes, they will resent you just because you stand between them and their abuser. It will be hard for you to understand. You will not be a replacement for their parents. Many times, you will be a bridge to their parents. Don't go into this thing thinking you will save them from their horrible life. You will be a first step to normalcy, to safety. You will offer them a warm bed and decent food. You will hold them when they cry and when they wake from nightmares, but most of these kids have a mom, a dad, a family that they love, and therein is the dilemma. Don't judge them. That job belongs to someone else. They will test you with bad behavior and watch for your reaction. Every eye roll from you or every sigh of exasperation you utter will be noted in their keen little minds. It will be the hardest thing you have ever done, but it will also be the most rewarding. I hope that helped to answer some your questions." Frank rose and smiled down at Cate. "Well I wish I could stay here all morning, but I have to get to work. Good luck with your decision-making." He walked to the counter to pay his bill, but Hannah waved him on.

"I've got this one, Frank," she called. "Have a good day!"

"Thanks, Hannah!" He shot back "you too" and was out the door.

Cate sat sipping her coffee and staring out the window. That conversation might have scared some people completely out of trying this crazy thing, but for Cate, it just reinforced her determination. Hannah brought the coffee pot around to refill her mug.

"I'm almost caught up," she told her. "I'll be with you in a few minutes." Cate looked around and observed the place had nearly cleared out, and she hadn't even noticed. A few minutes later Hannah, cradling her own mug of coffee, sat down to join her.

"That looked like a complicated conversation you were having with Frank," she mentioned as she glanced out the window nonchalantly. "Is it anything you can share?"

Cate gave her a blow-by-blow description of what was said and asked Hannah if she had come to a decision. "I made my decision yesterday. I think it's important. We should do it. I know that the majority of the burden will be on your shoulders because you will actually be in the house, but I will do whatever I can to help you. Grace and Michael can manage the bakery with some notice, and I could take on another part-time student if necessary. I could cover for you when you have to work, and I'll share the expenses. That being said, I totally understand if you don't want to do it. It's a lot to take on."

Cate smiled at Hannah. "Then I guess we should call Karen, tell her we accept, and find out what the next step will be. I'll call and let her know when I get home. I left her card on the dining room table. Do you want to come over after work? I could whip something up for dinner, or we could order takeout. I was also thinking that I should finish up the last bedroom sooner rather than later. I could pick up a couple of dressers, maybe another set of bunk beds. Should we have a supply of toys and books on hand, or maybe we should wait until we know who we're getting and what ages they are? What do you think?"

"I think you should back away from the coffee," said Hannah. "Let's, at least, wait until we speak with Karen, then we'll have a better idea of what to expect. I'd bet she has some kind of beginner's packet for newbies. Why don't you just go home and relax tonight. You have a couple of twelve-hour shifts coming up, don't you? You've been going at full speed for weeks now. I'll go home, catch up on some laundry, watch a little guilty pleasure TV, and we can get together on Friday. I am sure enough of my decision to leave the rest in your hands. If you feel the same way on Friday, call Karen and tell her we accept her proposition. Then come for breakfast at the bakery and let me know."

"That sounds like a completely rational solution. Why didn't I suggest that?" responded Cate. She placed five dollars on the table and hugged Hannah goodbye.

"Don't work too hard," she cried out as she exited.

She strolled home at a leisurely pace. When she arrived, she sat quietly in the living room for a while, then opted for lighting a fire and reading her book. She covered up in a cozy throw and leaned back to enjoy her book, but she dozed off in no time at all. She awoke an hour later and realized she must have been tired. As a rule, she wasn't one for napping. She ambled into the kitchen and decided on leftover soup and a piece of Hannah's delicious bread. While everything was out, she packed up a bowl for her lunch tomorrow and stowed it into the fridge. She climbed the stairs to finish up some laundry of her own. There were only two loads to do. She remade the bed in the yellow bedroom and then decided to soak in the tub and give herself a mani-pedi. She deserved a little personal pampering. It was still early, but she decided to retrieve her book from downstairs and make it an early night. She set her alarm for five and read until sleep claimed her.

She was awake half an hour before the alarm sounded. She readied herself for work, ran down to the living room and grabbed her portable pulse-ox from a bowl by the door and shoved it into her scrub top pocket. She then lifted her stethoscope from one of the hooks where she left it hanging and placed it around her neck, then scooted out the door to the bus stop. She arrived a few minutes early so stopped by the cafeteria for a cup of coffee and some oatmeal. After breakfast, she ran up to the fourth floor to check her assignment for the day on the whiteboard in the RT break room. Finding that she was covering the ICU, she went downstairs to the third floor to get the report from the overnight shift before starting her day.

The ICU was located at the end of a long white corridor in order to decrease random foot traffic in the area. Rooms appeared scary for family members on first arrival because of the copious amount of machinery in each room. Mounted on the wall close to the back of the room facing outward flashed an electronic box with multicolored waving lines and numbers all over its face. Many wires attached directly to a patient. One colored wavelength represented heart conductivity, the speed and shape of each complex spelled out a great deal of information for the physicians, and they were practiced at reading much of that information with only a glance at the monitor. Another colored line was a read out of art-line activity used to measure real-time blood pressures important in crisis situations. Flashing numbers represented SpO2 levels and respirations, and those numbers reflected how well a patient was oxygenating. These monitors beeped and alarmed incessantly, sometimes for a vital reason, sometimes not. Pulse oximeters that worked their way loose from fingers caused alarms, or even coughing or moving could cause a ventilator to make an awful racket. The uninviting hospital bed with plastic-covered mattresses stood front and center. The head of the bed could be raised and was usually kept up to at least 30 degrees and boasted bells and whistles of its own. The bed could be raised up while staff completed bedside care or lowered down for patient safety on a whim. It was equipped with IV poles, and most patients in an ICU setting required many IVs, sometimes six or seven or more, depending on the diagnosis. Each bed was also rigged with digital scale for patient weights, which became critical to document while so many IV fluids and medications were being pushed. Too much weight gain could signal fluid overloads. The bed even came fitted with an alarm of its own in case a medicated patient was trying to get out of bed. Each piece of equipment possessed a unique sound so staff could differentiate between them to determine quickly what it was that needed attention. Pumps to push medication in at a very specific dosage were also attached to IV poles. There were also pumps that would squeeze a patient's legs at a regular interval that helped to prevent blood clots for bedridden patients. Then to all this unfamiliar noise and busyness, they would enter to discover their loved one immobile on the bed, with so much medication on board that they can't respond and a tube in their airway to help them breathe from the ventilator in the corner. Any family member, upon entering this environment for the first time, would be justified to discover they were numb with fear.

Her day was very busy, consisting of taking several road trips with patients to radiology for CT scans, monitoring eight patients on ventilators, and two tracheostomy patients that needed frequent suctioning to keep their airways clear. She was also responsible for X-ray rounds where medical staff conferred over radiological findings from each patient chest X-ray and discussed positioning of the endotracheal tubes. Toward the end of her shift, she also was asked to extubate a young man that had been successfully weaning from his vent during the day. This was a pleasant task because once a patient is aware enough to be weaned from their medications, they were also aware enough to fight the tube helping them breathe, and most patients were extremely grateful to have it removed and to breathe on their own. It was always a good day for her when she ended her shift on a happy note. She then headed back to the RT station to get ready to report off to the next shift.

Her shift on Thursday mirrored her previous shift. She was again in the ICU. It was nice to be on the same unit because she already knew the patients. There were one or two new admissions since she left Wednesday but, for the most part, the same workload. She liked being busy. The hours passed faster, and she went through her day without ever thinking about her private life. She moved from one patient to another, one treatment to another all day, and then repeated the rounds. Staff and resident physicians alike discussed vent setting changes and endotracheal tube adjustments they wanted to make. Before leaving for the day, she always tried to go through each room, empty water traps, check tubing for condensation, and make sure supplies were properly stocked for the next shift because that's the way she liked to find things when she started in the mornings. After checking that patients and rooms were all in good shape, she went to her station for report.

Cate awoke the next morning intent on calling Karen. She knew deep in her soul that she was meant to open her home to children in need. That is why she met Hannah and why she was offered this house. With every fiber in her being, she was sure that she had been led to this place and this time, and she was ready to pull the trigger. She sprang from the bed and completed her morning routine. She dressed in jeans and a sweater and descended the stairs. It was too early to call Karen, so she brewed a pot of coffee and sat at the island with her steaming mug in her hands, staring into space, checking the time every few minutes. When eight o'clock finally arrived, Cate was already dialing. Karen answered after the third ring, sounding winded.

"Hi, it's Cate. Where do I sign?"

The next step was to arrange the training setup. It consisted of five levels. The more training one has, the more difficult the case they are prepared to handle. Some of the higher level of care (level 5) cases may be PINS, *Persons in Need of Supervision,* or JD, *juvenile delinquents.* It was suggested that she and Hannah just start in the beginning and increase the training as they felt comfortable. Preplacement training and initial licensing was the first step. This training included six hours of preplacement, thirty hours of licensure, and at least ten hours of ongoing training within the year more specific to the children in their care. They had to be fingerprinted and background checked. Cate's home was to be inspected for suitability. They embarked on the training while awaiting the results of the background checks. Some of the training were online modules of information to be read and followed by a quiz, and a video was included of a child that damaged the caregiver's home and destroyed some family heirlooms to cement the image of how difficult foster care can sometimes be, but both Cate and Hannah knew what they were signing up for.

By the end of the second week, everything was in place. The initial training was complete, background checks and inspections were passed. They felt ready.

CHAPTER 6

And So It Begins

Thanksgiving was only three days away, and Cate was planning the menu, except for the bread and the pies that Hannah was preparing at the bakery. Challah bread was a favorite of Cate's. It was a braided egg bread that was a beautiful addition to any holiday table. She hadn't been shy about requesting it. Hannah had invited the guests, and Cate wasn't even sure who was coming. *"Filling up the table"* was all the answer she got from Hannah. She kept changing her mind about whether she should go gourmet to impress or stick with her traditional fare, and in the end, she chose to make the things she always made for David, and she hoped her guests wouldn't be disappointed. She was roasting a stuffed turkey and baking a ham decked out in pineapple slices and cherries, Southern-style cornbread dressing, cranberry apple relish, deviled eggs, green bean almandine, pan-seared brussels sprouts with cranberries and pecans, and a mountain of mashed potatoes and turkey gravy. She had always made latkes and applesauce for David, a favorite of his, and she planned to whip those up as well. She also brewed a gallon of sweet tea and would have other beverages available—coffee, soft drinks, and wine choices. She didn't imbibe, but she certainly didn't mind if others enjoyed a drink or two.

She spent the whole morning preparing the things she could make ahead. What a kitchen! It was a pleasure to cook in and so roomy to prep in. Running from fridge to stove to pantry wasn't a chore at all in this environment; it was a joy!

Early in the afternoon, she drove to a wood furniture warehouse and purchased four comfy stools for the island and another set of bunks for the empty bedroom. She loaded the stools and brought them home, but the bunks were being delivered. She packed up Hanna's stools and returned them to the bakery before they closed.

"Do I ever get to know who's on the guest list?" she called over to Hannah.

"Anyone that comes in here with no plans," Hannah called back. "Hate the thought of anyone spending the holiday alone. I don't know who will show up. I figure just roast a turkey, turn the TV to football, and they will come!"

Cate laughed and shouted, "I hope we have enough food, you silly girl! I'm sending you out in the cold to scrounge for scraps if we don't."

Snow was whirling around in gargantuan wafting flakes by the time Cate reached home again, and it was already coating the ground in the light fluffy snow that snowman-building children delight in. She parked in the garage and entered the kitchen from the back, but she was walking through to the living room to light a fire in the fireplace when she caught a glimpse of the view from those long expansive windows across the room. *It was like living in a snow globe,* she thought—snow blowing all around her and those gorgeous tall evergreens on the lawn iced in white. She had been used to incredible views in her beach house, but *this* was something altogether different. It was dreamlike and fanciful, and she was enchanted. She lit the fire, but it couldn't compete. She turned her chair, window framing her view, and stared out into the evening. Darkness was falling, and in spite of the snow, the stars shone brightly, crisply, through this magical dance of winter. Mesmerized, she sat curled in a plush blanket and wished she could share this moment with David.

It was also her tradition to put up the Christmas tree soon after Thanksgiving so she could enjoy it as long as possible. She pulled out the decorations in the garage and stored them in the coat closet so they'd be conveniently located when she was ready. She might even cut her own tree this year. She was, after all, in Wisconsin. She was going to go all out with decorations. This house *screamed* holidays. It simply must be appeased!

The morning of Thanksgiving found Cate bustling around. She was a flurry of energy, moving from kitchen to dining room smoothly and efficiently. The table was beautifully set with a center-piece consisting of crudités served in an oblong silver tray so artistically arranged that it resembled a window box of colorful flowers, only hers included edibles—carrots, celery, broccoli florets, purple cauliflower, red and yellow pepper strips, cukes, cherry tomatoes, and delicately cut radishes that could have been mistaken for flowers, with triplicate dips carefully placed around. She'd brought a largish table in with an ample surface that could serve as a buffet today.

Each place setting was adorned with her best crystal. She used her everyday stoneware but draped the table with colorful linens and embellished it with glass serving dishes filled with pickles and olives and butter and the like. The table sparkled, and she was satisfied with the results. Soon she would fill the buffet with food, but she first needed to ready herself.

Hannah was coming in about an hour, so she ran upstairs to shower and dress. When she at last descended, she was attired in a velvety-cream-colored cashmere dress that hugged her curves grace-fully and a pair of pliable baby-soft doe-skin-colored leather boots. The front of her hair was pinned up at the crown in a curving golden barrette that had been a gift from David, but the rest hung down in honey-colored ringlets over her shoulders and down her back. Her makeup was impeccable but barely there. She was elegant, and it seemed effortless. Hannah was pulling into the driveway and appeared to have someone with her in the car. Cate went to open the door and saw that it was Frank, helping Hannah carry a big box.

"I'm earning my meal today." He laughed. "I've sold myself for the price of a turkey dinner…just call me Hannah's pack mule! Wow! You look…just…wow! Maybe I got the better end of this deal after all!"

Cate smiled and curtsied. "Why, thank you, kind sir, but don't even try. You can't make me blush."

He proceeded to place the box on the island. "There are all manner of goodies in this box. What can I do to help?" he asked.

"You can place the pies on the far end of the buffet and then just find a game on TV. Hannah told me if we offer turkey and football, people will come, so it must be true. Can I get you a beverage? Hannah, anything for you?"

"I'll have a coffee," Hannah replied, "but I'll get it. You've got enough on your plate." She giggled. "Get it…enough on your plate? Thanksgiving? I crack myself up."

Frank couldn't help but laugh, not because what she said was funny but because she was so pleased with herself for saying it. "That sounds good to me," he agreed, still smiling. "A couple of my buddies from the station are coming, and they were very appreciative of your invitation, Cate. Hannah told us about it at the bakery."

Cate smiled and winked at Hannah and answered, "Oh, absolutely, my pleasure. The more the merrier, right, Hannah? Everything is warming, ready for guests to arrive."

As if on cue, the doorbell rang. It sounded, and Cate realized she had not heard it ring before. Never even noticed she had a doorbell. She opened the door to Karen Martin holding a bottle of wine and was admittedly happy to see her.

"Karen, welcome. Come on inside. Thank you for the wine and thanks for coming. Hannah, how would you like to serve drinks all around?"

There were a few more folks coming up the pathway. Cate held the door open for two young men smiling and carrying a beautiful bouquet of autumn flowers.

"Are you Cate?" the first one asked, handing her the bouquet. Cate nodded, accepted the flowers, and stepped aside to allow them entrance. "I'm Jake. I work at the police station with Frank and that guy"—he pointed to a second man—"is Nobie. He's out of the fire department. We sure do appreciate the invite. Thank you, Ma'am."

"Please, just call me Cate. Thank you for the lovely flowers. I'm glad you could join us today. Do you know everyone?"

She learned that everyone was acquainted except Nobie and Karen, so she introduced the two of them and thought she noticed a spark of interest between them. Hannah was getting drinks, and everyone was chatting in front of the fire.

"So, Nobie, that's an interesting name. Is it a family name?"

He laughed genuinely and said, "I'm afraid not. It was originally supposed to be Noble, but the hospital misspelled it on the birth certificate. At first, my mother was going to make them change it, but it grew on her. So here I am…Nobie Ethan Ward." And he grinned as everyone chuckled.

Nobie was tall, six two or three, with a mop of unruly black hair and eyes so dark they were nearly black. He was around her age, Cate thought, maybe thirty. He was lanky and slim but sinewy and well-muscled, like a runner. His angular face emitted good humor and likability. He was a natural entertainer and kept the group laughing, and his buddies, both Frank and Jake, valued the camaraderie. *That says a lot about a man*, Cate thought.

Cate excused herself saying, "Why don't you enjoy the game while Hannah and I get everything ready. If anyone else shows up, just invite them in. I don't think we have a head count, but we have plenty of room and more than enough food."

Cate had also invited a couple, Mariana and Hector Ramirez, that she had met at work. Their son Aquila was in the ICU. He had traumatically injured his left arm and hand at work, crushing it in some kind of pressing machinery. He was being kept chemically sedated and didn't know they were even present, and they were from out of state, somewhere in Missouri. She thought a holiday meal would get their minds off their troubles for a few hours. Eliza, one of the other therapists that Cate worked with, was joining them, and she volunteered to drive the Ramirezes over and take them back to the hospital afterward, and they had just arrived. She and Hannah had placed everything out, and it seemed like every surface was filled with holiday fare. She went into the living room to introduce the new arrivals and asked everyone to come into the dining room and be seated.

"If anyone else comes, we'll squeeze them in." They all found places to sit around the table as they exclaimed over its beauty and the array of delectable food. "Would anyone like to say grace?" Cate asked.

"I'll do it," responded Frank as he reached for his neighbors' hands. *"Thank you for the bounty of this table, Lord, and the loving hands that prepared it. Thank you for the presence of our friends gathered around us today. Please keep Aquila in the palm of your hand as he heals and help make us ever mindful of our blessings. Amen!"*

"Amen," repeated several guests.

"That was lovely, Frank, thank you. Now, who wants to carve?" Nobie rose, claiming to be the ultimate expert. "Everybody just dig in before the food gets cold!" said Cate. "Don't be shy!"

Jake was surprised and excited to see latkes and applesauce, and Frank couldn't stop eating the deviled eggs. The conversation was lively, and the company couldn't have been more agreeable if the guests had been handpicked weeks in advance. Everyone was in a jovial mood and genuinely seemed to delight in the company they were in. Nobie kept the table in stitches with jokes, and he was showering a great deal of attention on Karen. Mariana and Hector looked at ease for the first time in a week. Eliza and Frank were busy trying a little bit of everything on the table and oohing and aahing their satisfaction over their favorites.

Jake kept flirting with Cate, laughingly telling her that he was in need of a wife that could cook and look good doing it. Without missing a beat, she retorted that she was looking for the same thing in a man. The meal was a big success, but despite the hearty appetites, there was a lot of food left over.

Cate determined that she didn't want all this food piled up in her fridge, packed up the majority, and it was decided that Eliza would drop half of it off at the ICU break room for the staff working the holiday, and Jake and Nobie would deliver the other half to the crew at the fire station.

"I only want to leave enough turkey for a couple of sandwiches and a slice of Hannah's pecan pie I didn't leave any room for," she stated matter-of-factly. "Does anyone want to take anything else home because I still have so much leftover?"

Everyone contributed to the cleanup, and the kitchen and dining room were neat and orderly in no time at all. Jake and Nobie thanked Cate and Hannah for their hospitality and took a huge amount of food to the car. Eliza was taking her booty back to the hospital and returning Mariana and Hector to their son's bedside. The others took their drinks into the living room to catch up on the progress of the game. Hannah was sipping a red wine and declaring how robust it was when the phone rang.

CHAPTER 7

Something Wicked

Across town, in a small rundown apartment complex, a drama was unfolding for eight-year-old Liam and his two sisters, Brianne and Bella. Booster, his mother's boyfriend, had informed them that their mom had gone out early in the morning hours for work, but Liam knew that was a lie. His mother didn't work. She couldn't function enough to carry on a conversation, much less hold down a job. Since Booster had moved in, she spent her days either high or passed out on the couch, locked in the bedroom, or serving as a punching bag. Liam cared for the girls on a daily basis, a job he devoted himself to and had assumed of his own volition. He tried to keep quiet and out of the way so as not to attract too much attention from Booster, so he spent hours with the girls in their room, reading the same book over and over again and entertaining them as best he could. He only ventured out in search of food, which was, in itself, a challenge when no one in this house shopped, or to the bathroom when necessary. There was little food in the house today, and the girls were fidgety and restless from being cooped up. They hadn't been to school for so long; Liam no longer knew what day it was. None of them had slept well, not only because of the lack of exercise they were receiving lately but also because Booster had been especially obnoxious during the night, yelling and bullying his mother for hours. Liam had found it necessary to pick his battles and had long since given up trying to shield his mother from Booster, in preference to keeping his sisters out of his reach. The more Liam drew his attention or angered him, the more Bella and Brianne paid the price. Booster preferred to subdue Liam's uncooperative nature by punishing the girls because, frankly, punishing Liam himself wasn't a deterrent as he'd keep coming back for more. Hurting the girls was the only way to keep him in line the way Booster saw it. He wanted Liam to jump to it when he was told to do something, and the best way to make that happen was to threaten his sisters.

"I think it's bath time," shouted Booster as he shoved the bedroom door open. He was lurching unsteadily and holding onto a bottle as he bellowed to Liam to take action.

"Bath time?" he questioned, unconvinced of the motive behind this suggestion. They haven't left the bedroom.

"What have I told you about questioning my authority?" he shouted again. "Brianne, come here and take off those pajamas!" She looked over to Liam for confirmation that she should comply, but that act made Booster angrier than ever. "I said it's time to take your baths! Come here now, both of you, or I'll take my belt off."

Both Bella and Brianne stepped gingerly through the door and followed Booster to the living room. They stepped out of their pajamas and stood in the center of the room as he leered at them. He slipped his belt from the loops and held it, doubled it back on itself and held in front of him, slapping one hand with it as though he were daring them to defy him.

"Run the bathwater for them," he ordered Liam. Then he sank back into the sofa and swilled some more liquid from his bottle as he ogled Brianne.

Liam slid into the little bathroom and began running the water for their baths. The bathroom also had a door at the opposite end of the room that led to his mother's room, and as the noise from the running water masked his movements, he crept into her room quickly, and reaching for the phone, he prayed that it wasn't shut off. Hearing a dial tone, he breathed a sigh of relief and dialed 911. He spoke softly and agitatedly and related that his sisters were in danger and gave his address, then instead of hanging up, he laid the phone arm on the table where the phone was stationed and walked back to the bathroom to peer out at Booster, who now appeared to be dozing on the sofa. Liam held his finger to his lips and signaled to the girls to get dressed. They put their pajamas back on, and Booster had not moved. Liam watched him for a moment to assure himself that Booster was still out, then whispered to the girls to find shoes and coats and go to Mrs. Obermyer, the neighbor two doors down to wait for him. They scrambled into their things and slipped out the door. The door clicked as it closed, and Booster roused.

"Where are my little chickies?" he slurred. He raised himself to his feet and glanced into the bathroom, but when he realized they weren't taking a bath, he pounded over to the bedroom and, inspecting the empty room, turned his rage on Liam. "Where are they?" he demanded as he pushed Liam into the door of the bedroom with such force it caused him to strike his head and bite his tongue.

"They've gone" was his only reply. Booster rampaged through the house looking for the girls and screaming at Liam when he didn't find them. "Where have they gone?"

"Mom came while you were sleeping and took them to go grocery shopping."

Booster turned on him and eyed him intently, studying his expression as he spat, "Your mom never came here…she's never coming here again…WHERE ARE THEY? You can keep the little one. I only want Brianne. She's a looker with that creamy skin and red hair. She's the prize for all this crap I put up with from you."

Liam stared him down with disgust and stated in a calm steady voice, "You'll never touch her as long as I'm alive."

That's when he took the punch to his face that sent him sprawling into the bedroom. Booster loped back into the living room for his belt, and he raised it up as high as he could to bring the stinging leather forcefully against the boy's chest. Liam turned over to protect his face and bore the brunt of several more blows across his back and shoulders. He was trying to maneuver away from Booster's swing when the door crashed open, and the police burst in and witnessed the scene of the boy scooting back away from his tormentor, while Booster swung the belt at him again and again.

*****

It was a social worker on call from Department of Children and Families asking if Cate was prepared to take three children. Length of stay was, as yet, undetermined. She inquired about pertinent information as she had been trained to do and was told they were a boy, eight years, named Liam; a girl, six years, named Brianne; and a girl, four years, named Bella. Liam had called the police station himself and asked for help keeping his mother's intoxicated boyfriend away from his sisters. The mother was believed to be at work, but social services needed time to assess the home situation and had removed the children temporarily for their safety. They were to be checked over by a medical team and could be arriving in as little as two hours. Cate stated that she was ready for them and hung up the phone.

"So it begins," she said to Hannah with anticipation and explained the call.

Karen looked at Frank and said, "We better leave Cate and Hannah to themselves. Too many adults might frighten the children, and they will be fragile enough tonight." Both she and Frank hugged their hosts and thanked them for a wonderful holiday meal.

Frank eyed Cate and said, "You've got this! If I can be of service in any way, just call." And he handed her his cell number. Karen said she would be available too if they had questions and then turned away and headed out of the door.

Cate turned to Hannah and smiled. "Let's go get the bedrooms ready," she said calmly. "How do you feel?" She asked as she led the way up the stairs. She went to the linen closet and took out sheets for the beds and towels to supply the guest bathroom.

"I feel just fine," Hannah responded, helping to carry bedding into one of the bunk bedrooms. Cate looked up to search her face and noticed for the first time today how great she looked. She was smiling her dimpled smile. She was wearing black slacks and a Christmas-red sweater. She'd stuck sparkling dangly silver earrings in her lobes and a delicate silver chain around her neck. Her crop of hair was poking out at wild angles as if powdery white feather flowers were sprouting from her head. It appeared both arranged and unintentional at the same time. It suited her, and she looked stunning. She finished it off with classic black pumps. Cate felt a pang of guilt that she hadn't mentioned it before now.

"You look fantastic today, Hannah," she said at last. "I had such a great time today, and I don't think I even told you how much I appreciate you. Thank you for managing all the pies and that delicious bread. Mostly though, thank you for your friendship. When I counted my blessings this morning, you were top of the list."

Hannah eyed her friend and spoke sincerely. "And I count you at the top of my list too, sister! Now stop getting so mushy. We have work to do!" Cate could not see that as she turned her back, there was a tear in her eye, and she was flushed. She was touched by Cate's words.

They made the bunks with sheets imprinted with little purple flowers and purple coverlets. Cate moved the fluffy white rug from the yellow bedroom and placed it by the beds. She then opened the closet to reveal a stash of clothes and toys and removed two small pink teddy bears from the overhead shelf and perched them atop the beds, one on each pillow.

"There," she said, perusing the room with satisfaction.

Hannah was staring at her in amazement. She asked in surprise, "Where in the world did you get all that stuff in the closet? I suppose the dressers are full too? I thought we were going to wait until we knew what each situation was? I could have helped with the expense."

"Remember when you came back from the store with items for Kendall?" she answered, "I was possessed by the same bug that got you. I couldn't resist. I've been stocking up for the past two weeks. I found most of the clothing in a resale shop in Madison. I didn't want the kids to snuggle with used stuffed animals, so I picked them up at Target. They can be therapeutic, don't you agree? We need to get Liam's room ready…then I need to show you the attic."

The attic, thought Hannah. *My stars, what in the world has she done now?*

They moved into the yellow bedroom and tried to decide how to make it more suited to a boy's taste. Cate brought out a Green Bay Packer bedspread for the bed, and since the walls were yellow, it looked as though it was intended for the room. She waffled on deciding whether to place a stuffed animal on his bed, but in the end, Hannah settled it by saying that he was only eight, and he could put it aside if he didn't want it. It would be worse to not give him the choice. So nestled on his pillow was a fuzzy brown bear with a green bow around its neck.

Cate led Hannah up into the attic and through the heavy wooden door that she now left ajar. Inside, she had installed metal shelving aligning one wall, with bold black labels on the face. On top of each shelf were clothes arranged by size and gender. She had shelf upon shelf of items. She had thought of everything, from pajamas to winter coats. Bins fitted on one shelf held gloves and hats and socks. Diapers were visible on another.

"I thought it would be better if I could *shop* right here. In case we needed to accommodate kids with no notice. The stores aren't always open, just like today. Am I crazy?" she murmured.

Hannah had to consciously keep her mouth from hanging open as she scanned the shelves. Everything was so neatly organized. It would be possible to come up here to locate an outfit for a three-year-old at a moment's notice or diapers and sleepers for a baby. Hannah was flabbergasted.

"When did you have time for all of this? And yes, you are most definitely crazy, but I love you for it!"

They crept down the stairs as Cate tried to sum up her actions for Hannah. "While we were completing the training, I started to worry about being prepared. It's always been a fault of mine, but I have to admit, it got worse after losing David so unexpectedly. I almost went over the edge. The accident happened. It was done, and I had no power to change anything. Life as I knew it changed in an instant. Since then, I have developed an undeniable need to control my surroundings as much as possible. That is going to be challenging in the future, and there is nothing I can do about it but to cushion my sanity. That *room* upstairs…*that* I can control. Most things I purchased are secondhand. I washed everything twice and made a few simple repairs before putting it on the shelf so the cost is minimal, comparatively speaking. Does that make sense?"

"It makes perfect sense. I understand completely. The idea of that room of yours is inspired. I would never have considered anything like it, but it's exactly the thing for what we are hoping to accomplish here. Today is a perfect example. Those kids might arrive with no belongings, and nothing is open today. What would we have done? You are too much for words, and I am in awe of you. Now make a pot of coffee for me before I curl up and die from lack of caffeine." Hannah always managed to turn a serious conversation around with her sense of humor. That was something else that Cate appreciated as she headed toward the coffeepot.

"Grab that pecan pie out of the fridge, will you, Hannah? I think I have room for it now," she drawled. They sat at the island, ate pie, and drank coffee, and Hannah commented on how much she liked the barstools. These were certainly an improvement over the little hard wooden ones that were borrowed from the bakery.

"I don't mind sitting in these at all." Hannah beamed. "They're kinder to my backside. Where did you get them?" The doorbell sounded. They gave each other a nod and strode over to open the door.

Cate swung wide the door and motioned for the group to enter. An older woman of about fifty or sixty entered, with three colorfully clothed sullen-looking children behind her.

"Hi, I'm Helen Crawford. I work for DCF, and these"—she stepped aside to introduce the children—"are Liam, Brianne, and Bella." She placed a hand on the shoulder of each child as she named them.

Cate smiled at Helen, but her attention was on the boy, Liam. His face was red on one side, and he had a black eye developing as well. She then took in the girls, and while they appeared to be okay physically, she could tell they were terrified of her. Liam stood between them, holding onto their hands. She looked at Hannah, and as if they were in sync, Hannah moved over to Helen to speak with her, while Cate kept her attention focused entirely on the children, taking in every detail.

She kneeled down to their level and said very quietly, "Hello, my name is Cate, and that lady over there in the red sweater is my friend, Hannah. We would like it if you could stay here with us for a little while. What do you think about that idea?"

"We can take care of ourselves, and I'm in charge," Liam answered her, glowering.

"I'm sure you can, Liam," Cate said patiently. "I can already see that you are an excellent big brother. How about if you take care of yourselves right here, until we make sure it's safe for you to go back home."

She saw him relax a wee bit, so she asked him if there was anything she could do for the girls, unsure if he would accept help from her for himself. He wanted to trust her, but he was very protective of his little sisters. Cate speculated that his life was watching out for them, and she admired his devotion. She waited patiently for his answer, smiling as she kept eye contact with him.

At last, he relented enough to say, "They haven't had lunch or dinner yet. It's been a bad day."

"Well then, you are in luck!" Cate said enthusiastically. "We had a holiday lunch today, and we have enough food for an army left, so would you like to go into the kitchen with me and help figure out what they might like? I'll bet you know all of their favorites, don't you, Liam?"

He nodded and gave Cate a hint of a smile, but he was still guarded as she led them into the kitchen.

"After we get you something to eat, I'll give you a tour of the house. Now, I can either tell you what's in there, or you can look for yourself, Liam. What will it be?"

He preferred to rumble around in the refrigerator himself. He pulled out some of the cut-up vegetables and dips and carried it over to the table.

Cate got out three plates, glasses, and some silverware, wishing she had thought to get children-sized dishes. These would do for now. She asked Liam if the girls liked milk, and he nodded, so she poured it into the three glasses saying, "They might eat better if you join them."

She got them all arranged at the table and saw that Bella was too small to reach the surface. She went into the living room to get her dictionary from the shelf. It was big enough to give her a little height if she sat on it. Another thing she should have considered, she admonished herself. Cate was just in time to thank Helen for bringing the children before she left. Hannah eyed the dictionary but never said a word as they started back toward the dining room together. When she arrived, she lifted Bella up and placed the dictionary onto her chair and then replaced her atop the dictionary. Success! The child could now reach her plate, and she smiled up at Cate. Hannah looked at the veggies and dip on the table.

"Would you like a turkey sandwich to go with your veggies?" she asked them. Liam said yes, but Bella and Brianne can share a sandwich, and they don't like crust.

"Okay," responded Hannah. "Mayonnaise or mustard?" She grabbed the ingredients from the fridge.

"Mayo," he answered.

Hannah prepared the sandwiches, cut one on the diagonal, and trimmed the crust off. She took them into the dining room and deposited them onto the plates before the children.

"Brianne really likes broccoli. She calls them trees," he shared. "Bella won't eat much of anything. She'll try it, but she just doesn't eat much. She does like those little cheesy fish crackers though."

"What do you like, Liam?" Hannah asked. "Do you have a favorite food?"

He thought about it for a minute and finally replied, "Maybe spaghetti...or pizza."

"Wow," responded Cate, grinning, "Pizza seems to be a very popular food in this house." They finished eating, and Bella announced that she had to pee. Cate looked down at Liam and asked, "Can she go alone, or does she need assistance?"

"No, she can go alone. She'll need help to reach the sink after, so she can wash her hands."

Keeping Liam included in the decision-making was putting him at ease. He was a font of useful information about the girls. They all waited by the bathroom door for her to finish and then Liam lifted her up to the sink. Hannah led the way up the stairs as Cate followed behind. She started with the bedroom intended for the girls. They loved the purple beds, but the pink teddy bears were the big hit. Bella scooped up the one from the bottom bunk and cuddled it in her arms. Brianne was excited about sleeping in the top bunk and climbed up to claim her bear. Liam explained to her that she wasn't to jump or stand in the top bunk.

"It's just for lying down," he said seriously, and she nodded her assent. Then he looked to Cate and asked, "Where is my bed?"

"It's right next door," said Cate and led him in to the next room. He liked the Packer bedspread and looked all around the room. He actually patted the teddy bear on his pillow, and Cate was glad Hannah suggested it.

"This is really a nice room, but it won't work," he said. "I'm too far from them." He pointed to his sisters.

"They'll be safe here," responded Cate. "And you'll be in the next room to make sure."

He didn't say anything, but he didn't look convinced. She showed them to the bathroom and let them open all the doors to see where things were located. She had not seen a single bag when they had come, so she thought she would check the labels in their clothes while they were bathing to choose a few things for them in the *attic store*. She had placed a night-light in the receptacle in the bathroom so they could find their way in the night. She asked if they were ready for baths, and Liam answered that Brianne and Bella could bathe together, and he would take his afterward. Cate handed them a basket to deposit their dirty clothes into and bent over the tub to run a bath for them.

She studied them as the water filled the tub. The girls she likened to porcelain dolls. Their skin was creamy pale, and they each had a head full of curly red hair, the color of a glowing fire. Their eyes were as blue as a cornflower, and they wore a worried, expectant expression that saddened Cate. If not for the fact that Brianne was a smidge bigger, they could have been twins, and Cate imagined that they were mistaken for such, in spite of the size difference. Liam was red haired and freckle faced, and Cate thought too serious for one so young. She had to wonder what the home life was like to have taken his childhood and turned him into a miniature adult.

The tub had sufficiently filled, and the girls stripped off their clothes and put them in the basket. Cate helped them into the tub, while Hannah checked the sizes. Hannah inquired if Liam knew what size he was, and he said he wore size 8, just like his age. So Hannah ran up to the attic to choose pajamas and clothes for tomorrow. When she came down, she handed the pajamas into the bathroom and went to place the clothing into the chests in each of the bedrooms. She had chosen three outfits for each child, including socks and underwear. Cate helped the girls into their PJs and steered them out of the bathroom so Liam could bathe. He was reluctant to be parted from them at all, so Cate left the bathroom door open so he could hear them.

She and Hannah sat on the floor outside the bathroom door and brushed and braided the girls' hair. Cate took care of Brianne, and Hannah took care of Bella. By the time they were done, Liam had completed his bath and dressed in his pajamas. In place of slippers, they all wore fuzzy socks. Cate put the basket of clothes by the laundry room door for tomorrow and asked if anyone wanted a snack and an hour of TV before bed. The girls squealed, and Liam had to admit he thought it was a capital idea.

They were lucky enough to catch *Finding Nemo* on and sat down to relax as they snacked on apple slices and peanut butter. Cate was seated in one of the cub chairs, Liam was sprawled out on the rug in front of the TV, and Hannah was buried under red-haired angels on the sectional, one on either side of her.

When the movie finished, Cate called out, "Bedtime! Who wants a story?"

While Hannah read *Green Eggs and Ham* to the girls, making them laugh out loud with her antics and expressions, Cate asked if there was anything Liam wanted to discuss with her or if he had any questions about what was going on that he needed to ask. He shook his head emphatically, so Cate let him choose a book from the bookshelf to read. He chose *Harry Potter and the Sorcerer's Stone*, and Cate read out the first chapter, then gave him a good night kiss on the forehead, said goodnight, and went in to say good night to the girls.

She and Hannah padded downstairs quietly and sat in the living room to talk.

"So far, so good," whispered Hannah. "Those girls are absolutely adorable."

"I know, aren't they? And Liam is trying so hard to be a little man, when he should be thinking about toys and sports."

Hannah had to leave as she was opening the bakery in the morning, and she thanked Cate for the wonderful meal and insisted that she call at any hour if trouble arose. Cate locked the door behind her, sat down, and stared into the fire, revisiting the events of the day. After about an hour, she climbed back up the stairs, showered, and slid into her own bed. She was weary but fulfilled and drifted off into a dreamless sleep.

Cate woke with the dawn and lay still for a moment to gather her thoughts, then she suddenly recalled that she wasn't alone in the house. She listened but heard no sounds. She rose from the warm bed and padded into Liam's room to peak in on him, but he wasn't there! She felt panic rising in her and went next door to check on the girls. There he was, on the floor of the doorway, with his blankets and the brown bear, sound asleep. The girls were sleeping as well. *He's guarding the door*, Cate thought.

She turned into her bathroom to brush her teeth and wash her face, trying to stay as quiet as possible. Then she shuffled down to the kitchen to brew coffee and peruse the fridge for breakfast ideas. Staring into the fridge wasn't filling her with inspiration, so she closed the door, poured a cup of coffee, and decided to wait for the children to wake and let them have a say in what they wanted to eat. She had hardly finished her first cup when she started to hear some noise upstairs. Torn between hurrying to help them and giving them some privacy, she decided to stay where she was and give them a little space. This whole situation had to be taking a toll on them, especially Liam.

When the children came bounding down the stairs, they were already dressed, faces scrubbed, and teeth brushed. The girls still wore the braids from last night, but Liam's hair was freshly combed and still wet where he attempted to tame it. He must be practiced at looking after the little ones. His eye was dark purple and swollen this morning, and his cheek was still angry and red.

"Good morning, everyone." She checked out Liam's face. "Is your eye hurting this morning? I can get you an aspirin," she offered.

He shook his head. "No, I'm fine, thanks," he answered.

"Would you like to tell me how you got that shiner?" she asked.

He shook his head again.

"Okay, I'm here if you change your mind. What would you like for breakfast?"

"Toast?" questioned Liam.

"And jelly!" added Brianne. "The grape kind."

"You got it, but is that all? Do you want some eggs or an omelet? I can put ham and cheese in it," she added.

"That sounds good, if you don't mind making it. We don't ever have omelets. I don't know if Brianne or Bella will eat it," he muttered.

"Well, let's find out. Who wants to help?" Cate shouted and got a resounding "Me!" from each of them.

She got all of her ingredients and placed everything on the island to prep. She assigned Liam to grating the cheese with a box grater, and he seemed to be enjoying the job. Brianne got to crack the eggs, and Bella got to stir. They were all very excited about helping. Cate cut up some ham on the cutting board and let each child have a bite as she chopped. She showed them how to coat the pan with a little olive oil and pour the scrambled eggs into the pan, then she let Brianne and Bella add some ham pieces and allowed Liam to sprinkle in the cheese. She left it on the burner for a minute while she got down some plates and threw some bread in the toaster. She next got some silverware and glasses and turned the omelet with a flip, causing the girls to cheer. She again let it sit on the burner and poured milk and placed butter and grape jelly on the countertop. Then she poured the omelet out onto a dish, cut it into thirds, and gave each child a portion. By the time the toast popped up, she was ready with a little butter and jelly. The whole ordeal only took a few minutes. Everyone got to participate, and the kids were all enraptured with the experience, even Liam. Bella left some on her plate, but she ate over half, and the other two cleaned their plates.

Cate allowed them to choose a TV program while she cleaned the kitchen. Little Bella scurried up the stairs and returned again, carrying all three teddy bears. They camped out in the living room, watching *Sesame Street*. She was nearly finished with the dishes when the phone rang.

It was Karen, calling with an update. The boyfriend has been arrested for assaulting a child, and for the moment, the mother is more upset about the boyfriend than the kids. The investigation would be ongoing, and the children would be staying with Cate until further notice. After the kitchen was cleaned, Cate ran upstairs and dressed in jeans and a sweatshirt.

She went up to the attic store and grabbed some mittens and scarves and hats for the kids. Then she bounded down the stairs and put the winter gear on hooks above the bench in the entryway. She joined the children on the sectional, and they reclined on each side of her as they did last night with Hannah. Even Liam stretched out on one end. When *Sesame Street* was over, Cate asked if anyone wanted to build a snowman, and everyone jumped to their feet in excitement.

She made sure each child was properly bundled up in winter gear, and out they went. She showed Liam how to roll a smallish snowball into a larger one, and he proceeded to roll the snowball around the yard until he could no longer thrust it forward.

"It seems this is where he wants to live." Cate laughed. They started to roll up a smaller one for the middle and, finally, the last. They stood by and inspected their work. Bella proclaimed it was the best snowman in the world! Cate whispered confidentially, "Oh, Bella, it's not finished yet. Will you and Brianne promise to stay inside the gate with Liam while I run inside to fetch a few things?"

Bella and Brianne nodded most emphatically and bounced up and down in anticipation. They were being children, playing and laughing, and for a little while, they hadn't a worry in the world, and it did Cate's heart good to witness it. She ran inside to grab her camera, and she also rounded up a scarf and hat, a few pieces of charcoal from the garage, and a carrot from the fridge. She placed the snowman things in a bag and returned back to the yard. She handed the bag to the children and let them add the adornments as they wished, while she stood well back and snapped photos.

Liam was directing, and the girls' eyes were filled with wonder over the end result. They squealed and giggled and danced all around their little creation. *This,* thought Cate, *is one of the good days.* And she filed this scene in her mind to bring up in her memory when the days weren't so good. She watched for a little longer and then noticing how pink the children's faces were from the cold, she suggested they go inside to warm up, and the children reluctantly filed in behind her and shed the winter trappings in the entryway, hanging them up on hooks to dry out. Cate suggested they stand by the fire and warm their hands and faces for a little while, and she turned toward the kitchen saying, "I'll make us some cocoa, and we can sit in the dining room and color. I think I have a gigantic box of crayons and a stack of coloring books."

Bella and Brianne glanced at each other and grinned. Liam studied his sisters and looked after Cate with appreciation in his eyes. Cate placed the mugs of cocoa on the table, called for the kids to come in, and went in search of the coloring supplies in the office.

As she was on her way back into the dining room, she heard a crash and ran into the room in time to see that Brianne had dropped her cup. Cocoa and shards of ceramic from the mug were everywhere, but as Cate ran in, Brianne had thrown her little arms up as if to protect her head. Bella and Liam stood stock still, with large eyes and gaping mouths, waiting for a reaction, and in that instant, Cate understood that they expected to be punished, and she could only imagine how. She forced herself to slow down and, when she reached Brianne, saw that she was crying.

"I didn't mean it," she cried. "It was hot, and I dropped it. I'm sorry. I should have waited. I'm sorry!"

As Cate neared her, Liam was on his feet in an instant but wasn't close enough to reach her. Cate squatted down and raised Brianne's face up gently with her fingers and looked deeply into her eyes.

"*This,*"—she pointed to the cocoa and remnants of the mug on the floor—"*This, is just stuff.* It's a little mess that we can clean up in a minute. That mug can be replaced. You are what's important here! Are you okay? Do you have any cuts or burns?" She searched Brianne's hands for damage.

Liam stopped suddenly and stared at the scene in disbelief. Then his demeanor changed physically. As Cate looked to each child to reassure them, she witnessed the change in Liam. His squared shoulders relaxed, and his troubled expression softened and then he smiled…his smile seemed to encompass the whole of his face, and he returned to his seat and happily sat down.

Cate instructed everyone to stay in their seats until the mess was cleared away. She picked Brianne up and took her into the kitchen and sat her down on the counter by the sink. She extracted a hand towel from a drawer and dampened it to wash the tears from the little girls face. She examined her hands more carefully to make sure.

"You are much too pretty for tears! Let's wash them away," said Cate softly. She returned Brianne to her chair in the dining room, made sure there were enough crayons and coloring books to spread around, and finally, she began to sweep up the shattered cup and deposit the pieces into the trash. She took out a mop and tidied up the floor, then turned to Brianne and smiled. "See, no problem at all."

She left them to color, and stepped into the kitchen to make a call, and when she returned, there was artwork galore to be appreciated. She posted the pictures all over her refrigerator, much to the delight of the children.

"It's time to think about lunch. Any suggestions?" Cate inquired.

They settled on grilled cheese sandwiches and tomato soup and gobbled it all down, chattering and sharing stories with each other. When they had finished eating, Cate directed the girls that a nap was in order. Liam was allowed to read in his room if he didn't want a nap, and Cate admitted that she had a treat in mind for this afternoon, but it was to be a surprise. Off they went, climbing up to wash their face and hands, and crawl in for a nap. After about fifteen minutes, Cate followed them up to peak in and make sure they were resting. The girls were bright cheeked and snuggled in with their bears in dreamland. She turned to Liam's room, and when she stuck her head in, he glanced up from *Harry Potter* and invited her in.

"Can we talk?" he asked tentatively.

"Of course," she replied. "You can always talk to me."

"Thank you for letting us stay here," he began. "My mom has boyfriends. None of them are great, but this one is bad, real bad. He drinks all the time, and I think he's gonna hurt Brianne. That's why he hit me. I wouldn't let him go into her room when she was taking a nap. I don't like the way he looks at her. My mom doesn't look out for them as much as she should. The girls had fun today, didn't they? We never made a snowman before. That was cool, and the cup thing… that was cool too. Thank you for that."

"Would someone have hit her for that?" Cate queried carefully. "I got the feeling she was expecting a slap."

"Oh yeah," he acknowledged. "We would all get a beating for that kind of thing. I was kind of surprised when you didn't get upset."

"Liam," Cate replied purposely, "it is *never* okay to hit a child. I personally don't believe we should hit anyone. If anything, we need to spread some love around. I can promise you one thing absolutely, as long as you and your sisters are in this house, you don't have to fear for your safety or for theirs."

"I wish we could live here forever," he said under his breath. And Cate imagined that her heart would crack into pieces resembling that broken mug from this morning.

"If you aren't tired, why don't you come downstairs and help me with the surprise for this afternoon?"

They crept down the stairs together, and Liam followed Cate to the coat closet where she handed him a box and directed him to place it on the floor in the living room and come back for another until all the boxes had been transferred to the living room. Cate peered out the window and recognized Frank's car pulling into the drive, with a monster of a Christmas tree attached to the top.

Liam followed her gaze and said with excitement, "Oh, cool! We're going to decorate a Christmas tree!"

Cate moved the club chairs toward the walls on either side of the windows and removed the table into the office space to make room for the tree. While she had accomplished that, Frank had wrestled the tree from the hood of his car and was pulling it up the paver walkway to the door. Liam scrambled to open the door for him.

Frank bellowed, "Where do you want it, Cate? It's a beauty! I picked it out myself! Do you own a tree stand? I can go buy one if you don't." Cate and Liam were both laughing at him. He was as giddy as a child at play.

"Liam, I'd like you to meet my good friend, Frank." Turning to Liam, she said, "Frank, this is my good friend, Liam"

They shook hands, Frank's hand completely obscuring Liam's by sheer size. Cate turned to Frank and thanked him for taking the time to pick up a tree. She explained that one thing she kept forgetting to address was car seats and bumper seats for the children, so she felt it wouldn't be safe to drag them out in the car without being properly prepared. She asked Frank how much she owed him for purchasing and delivering it for her as she pulled the tree stand from one of the bigger boxes and held it out to him.

He grinned and answered, "Dinner, and you have to let me help decorate it."

"Deal!" she retorted cheerily. "How about a cup of coffee for starters?"

As she turned toward the kitchen she noticed two adorable redheads peeking around the door, and she pretended to chase them with outstretched fingers in a tickling gesture. The girls screeched and giggled and ran the other direction as Cate cried out, "Frank, these two little munchkins are Brianne and Bella."

And she chased them around and back into the living room, where they suddenly stopped and gawked in amazement at the tree on the floor. They performed their little excited bounce that Cate reveled in watching. The "bounce" consisted of both girls standing side by side like little redheaded bookends, feet together, bouncing on the balls of their feet without ever leaving the ground, up and down again, all the while clapping their hands silently and beaming as if lit up from the inside, remarkable flaming curls rising and falling all around them. It was a magical sight to see, and as Frank watched them bounce, he lost his heart to them immediately.

"Well, girls," he said, smiling, "I guess we have a Christmas tree to decorate. Liam, do you think you could help me get this tree into the stand?"

Cate gazed into the room and thought she couldn't have asked for even one thing more. Her heart was full.

Cate left the busy scene to fetch a cup of coffee for Frank, and Karen's words kept entering her mind. *This is a family home,* and truer words couldn't have been spoken. She poured a mug for Frank and one for herself and strolled back to the living room. Hannah had arrived and let herself in. Frank and Liam had the tree up in the stand, and they were trying to determine if it was listing to one side. As she walked in behind them, every one of them were standing, examining the tree with their heads angled to the left. It was a comical sight and made Cate snort with laughter.

"Here's your coffee, Frank," she said as she handed him the mug. "Its fresh brewed if you want some, Hannah. I thought I would pop some corn, and we can make garlands for the tree. Would you and Liam like to tackle the lights, Frank? They're somewhere in one of these boxes." Liam began digging in boxes, searching for the one that contained the lights, and Hannah and the girls started for the kitchen. "How was your day?" she asked Hannah.

"It was great, but I couldn't wait to get back here and see Liam and these girls again," she answered gleefully. "And I must have been reading your mind, Cate, 'cause I brought a bunch of gingerbread cookies from the shop, and they will look terrific hanging on the tree. We can tie some up with ribbon, and the whole room will smell like Christmas." She looked at the tiny faces looking up at her. "What do you think, girls? Popcorn garlands and gingerbread ornaments… that's a lot to do. Do you think we can get it all done?"

Bella's and Brianne's eyes brightened in anticipation as they sat at the table with Hannah, while Cate popped a big pot of popcorn. She set it aside to cool and searched the pantry for red and green ribbons. Having no luck locating ribbons, she took some yarn from a craft bag in her office and decided it was an even better idea. Hannah had punched out little holes on the top of each cookie before baking for just this purpose. The girls helped by sliding a piece of yarn through each hole, then Hannah tied a little knot and, presto, instant ornaments. The popcorn garland proved to be too challenging for such small hands, so they hurried back into the living room to watch

Frank and Liam finagle the lights, while Hannah and Cate strung the popcorn.

"How was the night?" asked Hannah at last. "I saw the snowman outside, and it's a great addition to the yard."

"It's been completely wonderful. I did have a conversation with Liam that I'd like to share with you and Frank, but it'll have to wait until the kids are in bed. These children are a delight to have around, and I get the feeling that it's because of Liam. He's taken on the role of caregiver, and I tell ya, Hannah, he's done an incredible job. He's an eight-year-old adult. My guess is he's had to be."

The popcorn garlands were completed, and they took them to the tree for hanging. With Frank's help, Hannah strung the garland all around, and everyone helped to place the gingerbread men on the limbs. Cate opened a box full of ornaments, and each child took turns hanging them on the branches.

"Remember to put some on the back of the tree so we can see them from the window," Hannah called.

Cate picked up her camera and started to snap photos again. It wasn't dark yet, but the kids wanted to see the tree with the lights on, and Liam got the honor of switching the tree on because he had helped so much with the lights. When he flipped the switch, everybody gasped. The girls bounced and clapped their approval. They dashed outside to peek into the windows to see if it looked as good from the outside, and because it was so cold out, dashed right back inside chortling.

Cate mentioned that dinner time was drawing near and asked if everyone liked chili. Getting a firm yes, she started dinner.

After dinner came bath time and reading for the kids, and when everyone was tucked in for the night, the adults sat around the dining room table to chat. Cate shared the details of Liam's concerns with Frank, especially his concern for Brianne, and asked if he knew where the investigation stood at this point. He explained that he wasn't involved in the investigation, but that tomorrow, he would try to find out where things stood. He believed that if Liam would repeat his allegations to the investigating officer, it would go a long way toward keeping the assailant out of the house. He agreed to call tomorrow with an update, and even though she felt it was too much pressure to put on a kid, Cate promised to talk to Liam about formally speaking with an officer.

On another note, she said she needed to get car seats and boosters, in case she needed to take the kids somewhere in the car. "There is a shop in the children's hospital that sells them and teaches how to install them properly as well. I need to get over there next time I work."

It was getting late, so everyone said goodnight. Frank promised to call with updates on the investigation as soon as he knew anything, and Hannah said that she'd be back before dinner with an overnight bag and a movie. Everyone hugged, shared good night wishes, and they were off.

Since it was winter break, Michael and Grace had both been happy to pick up some extra hours, and so Hannah was planning to stay over on a couple of nights and take care of the children while Cate worked day shift on Friday and Saturday. She had even volunteered to sleep in one of the bunk beds in the extra room, and the children were looking forward to her stay. Hannah's plan to watch *Frozen* and bake cookies was a big hit. When she finally arrived that evening, she was assailed by hugs and kisses from both girls. They adored Hannah, and she was smitten by them as well. Liam was still a little distant, but who could blame him. Hannah wasn't about to push him. It was hard for him to trust, but he was coming along. He respected her relationship with his sisters, but he was ever watchful, even now, with everyone but Cate. Hannah allowed the girls to choose a book after their baths were complete, and they were ready for bed. They picked *Where the Sidewalk Ends* because they loved the "Hug O' War" poem.

Bella sang out "I will not play at tug o'war" answered by her sister's "I'd rather play at hug o'war," and they giggled and shrieked, "Everybody wins, everybody wins!"

"Hail Shel Silverstein, you've written one heck of a book," acknowledged Hannah as she watched the girls frolic and laugh and bounce. Oh, how she loved that bounce! She struggled with it because she so enjoyed watching them at play, but she managed to quiet them down and get them tucked into bed. She kissed each girl on the forehead and ambled into the spare room to read.

Cate was already in her room since she had to work in the morning. Liam had been reading *Harry Potter* in his room and listening to Hannah read to Bella and Brianne, and when she left them and went to her own room, he knocked on her door. She was surprised to see him there and asked if he was okay. He replied that he was fine but that he wanted to thank her for being so good to his sisters.

"They like you a lot, and you make them happy."

Hannah smiled at him and explained that they all, including him, made her happy and that she liked them too. The swelling was going down in his face, but his eye was still black and purplish. She wasn't sure how he would take it, but she kissed him on the forehead too and wished him sweet dreams. He turned and headed back into his own room so she didn't witness his grin.

CHAPTER 8

Fury and Defeat

Cate arrived for work a little before seven, and upon learning that she was assigned to the pediatric ICU, she left to walk over to that unit which was across the skywalk and up to the fourth floor. Reports in ICUs were generally given and received on the unit as opposed to the general care report in the department. When she arrived, the night-shift staff were scrambling to catch up from an admission that had arrived just hours earlier. She was checking with the night therapist to see if she could be of assistance. When she stuck her head into room 3 to ask, she inadvertently glanced at the patient in the room and suddenly felt there was something very familiar about her. Her offer of help was declined as Moira, the therapist, said she was nearly finished and would be out in a few minutes, and Kevin, the float therapist, was already assisting. Cate shook off the uneasy feeling that was shadowing her and walked over to the RT desk to copy a schedule on which to jot down notes about each patient from report. That was when her blood drained from her face, and she sat stone still staring at the name of the patient in room 3.

Kendall Campion—age 5, orbital fractures, mandible fractures, collapsed left lung, left radius fracture, left ulnar fracture, bruised kidney, left tibia-fibula compound fractures and, worst of all, possible traumatic head injury TBD—"to be determined." Cate was stunned, disbelieving, and it was a few minutes before she could function. She was on her way back to the room when Moira, the night-shift thera pist, who was exiting the room noticed that something was definitely wrong with Cate. She was as pale as death.

Moira hurried over and asked, "Are you well? You look as though all the blood has drained from your body. What can I do?"

"I'm fine," muttered Cate almost incoherently. "I know that child. She stayed in my home for a few days last month. What can you tell me? What happened to her? I need to sit down for just a minute."

She then walked back and lowered herself into a rolling chair by the desk. Moira shared what little she knew, but Kendall had only arrived about two hours ago. The docs had worked to stabilize her enough for a much-needed trip to CAT scanner in order to determine the damage. They were packing everything up right now for the road trip. Kevin, one of the float night shifters, was going to accompany them before he left for the day, and that's when they came rolling out of her room, moving urgently, on their way down to radiology. Cate only got to see her for a moment as they passed the RT station on the way to the radiology department, but she could see that Kendall was tubed and horribly bruised and battered. Her bed was filled to capacity with a plethora of equipment, oxygen tank, and monitors, and Kendall appeared so small and helpless. Cate simply could not believe what she was seeing. Everything was supposed to be okay. She was supposed to be in good hands! What had happened! At least, she was working today and could follow her progress. Oh, if she hadn't been working today, she might never have even known! Maybe there would be updates throughout the day. She needed to find out as much as she could. Cate forced herself to calm down, and to listen to report.

There were four other patients in the ICU today, and she must focus on the details and stay sharp. Keeping busy was always what got her through crisis, and crisis was something she had plenty of experience with. She began her rounds. She wanted to be especially efficient today so she could spend a little time with Kendall when she arrived back on the unit. She busied herself giving treatments and checking vent settings. It was her priority to assess each patient. She knew that nothing compared to laying eyes on a patient. You could *see* when a patient was working too hard to breathe or when their fingers were turning blue. You could *see* when tubing was working itself loose, but a monitor would only alarm after it had fallen off. Some people assessed by what the monitor readouts suggested, but she had seen monitors fail often enough that she used them for confirmation, not assessment. It was amazing what an experienced eye could pick up, and if you took the time to properly assess, you would be much more likely to notice subtle changes in your patients' status.

Cate was occupied with rounds, treatments, then stocking, but Kendall still had not returned. If it had been only a head CT scan, it would have been quicker, so she assumed they must be evaluating more than the head injury.

Nearly three hours later, Kendall returned to the ICU. Cate entered her room to assist her counterpart in hooking all the equipment back up. She spoke briefly to Kevin about the case, and he reported that the scan had not been officially read, but the chatter from the docs wasn't good. At this point, no one expected her to recover. Cate looked down into Kendall's face and could see only a hint of the child she knew under all the bruised multicolored swelling.

She bent down low and stroked her hair as she whispered through her tears, "I didn't know! I would have done more, but I didn't know. I'm so sorry that I didn't protect you from this."

All she could do now was to wait and pray for some improvement. She gave Kendall the best care she could offer and waited. It was close to one o'clock before Cate would allow herself to leave the unit, and instead of going for lunch, she called Frank. He came on the line right away as if he had been awaiting her call.

"I guess you know," he queried.

"Know?...*Know what Frank?* I get to work this morning to find the precious little girl that shared my home for a few days last month has been beaten until she is completely unrecognizable. What happened this time, Frank? Where is her mother now?" Anger got the best of her, and she vacillated between fury and defeat. She was on the edge of losing it.

"You took the bus in to work this morning, didn't you? What time will you get to leave? I'll come to pick you up out front to take you home, and we can discuss everything I've been able to learn then. You should know that Jenny is dead, and Margie had just gone back to Cedar Rapids two days ago. She is on her way back again now. I don't think she will arrive until around six."

She was completely deflated. "Thanks for telling me, Frank. I get off at three," she said at last. "I'll wait for you in front around three fifteen. I have to go back."

There had been no change in Kendall's condition. Her doctors were waiting for her grandmother to arrive before making any other decisions for her care.

Cate rounded on her patients once more before her shift ended, then spent the last half hour sitting by Kendall's bed holding her hand. She kissed her forehead and left to give report to the incoming shift. It turned out to be her friend Eliza. Cate briefly explained her relationship with Kendall. She left her number and asked that Eliza give it to Margie Campion when she arrived, along with the message to call if she needed anything and that Cate would return in the morning otherwise. Eliza agreed to relay the message when the timing was appropriate. Cate thanked her and walked downstairs to meet Frank by the front entrance. He was already waiting in his unmarked police car when she exited the building. He waited for her to buckle up and eased the car out into traffic to exit the hospital drive.

"I don't know what to do with all this anger," she said bitterly. "It's just so senseless. What kind of animal injures a helpless child, and why didn't we recognize her danger?"

"We didn't recognize her danger because Jenny protected him," Frank answered gently. "We now know that she didn't fall down the stairs to the laundry room last month. She was pushed. He would have gone after Kendall next, but she slipped out the door before he could find her and got away from him. This time, he shot Jenny twice in the chest and threw Kendall into a wall. The neighbors called us when they heard screams and gunshots. When we arrived, he was sitting in the recliner, drinking a beer and watching ESPN. He didn't even try to deny it. It turns out that he had been gone almost all night, and Jenny had locked him out of the house. When she wouldn't let him in, he broke a plate glass window and entered through the broken glass. We had to handcuff him in order to get to Kendall and her mother. Jenny was pronounced dead at the scene, and we found Kendall in a heap on the bedroom floor. We arranged transport for Kendall to Children's, and you know the rest."

"Does Hannah know?" she asked dismayed. "She was really taken with Kendall. This'll break her heart."

"I haven't talked to her," he replied. "I'll go in with you and keep the kids occupied while you fill her in."

Cate and Frank entered the house to find the whole gang camped out in the living room, totally engrossed in Frozen. Hannah was in the middle of the sectional, Bella on one side, Brianne on the other, which was their normal pose whenever watching TV with Hannah. Liam, lying on the floor, turned and nodded as Frank took his seat in one of the empty club chairs. Liam looked up to Frank, and Cate felt he was just the role model the child needed at this stage of his life and was grateful of his presence. Hannah glanced up and noticed almost immediately there was something odd in Cate's manner. She suggested to the children that this was the perfect time to pause the movie and take a potty break.

"Everybody off," she challenged. "There's a bathroom for everyone in this house! Go to it!" She smiled at them as they each scampered away in answer to her request. She turned to Cate and demanded, "I can see it in your face. Tell me what's wrong?"

"Let's step into the office and talk. Will you start the movie for the kids when they get back?" she asked Frank, and when he bobbed his head in assent, Cate followed Hannah into the office and closed the door behind her.

Frank kept an eye out for the kids to join him but also watched Hannah from the chair. Her expression changed from horror to anger to grief in a matter of minutes, and Cate reached out to comfort her as she began to cry.

"I have to go see her right away," Hannah sobbed. "Do you mind if I leave for a while?"

"Of course you want to see her," Cate replied. "We can tell the children that something came up, and you need to leave to take care of it. I understand completely. Maybe her grandmother will be there by the time you arrive. Call me if I can do anything and keep us posted of her condition if you are able. I wish I could go with you."

Hannah composed herself and opened the door just as she heard both girls running back into the living room. "Girls," she said, "I've just learned from Cate that I have a sick friend in the hospital, and I'm going to go see if there is anything I can do for her. Frank and Cate will finish the movie with you, but you'll have to tell me all about it when I get back. Is that a deal?"

"Yes," answered Brianne, "but you're gonna miss the best part."

Bella reached up to pat her hand, and the gesture reminded her so much of Kendall she almost started to cry again. She gave them each a kiss on the forehead and stepped out into the cold crisp air and found her way to her car, fighting the tears all the way.

Liam's gaze followed her as she closed the door. He looked at Cate, and then Frank, but was reluctant to ask any questions, as if he knew there was a problem but wasn't sure if he wanted to know what it was. He was only eight but already the champion of picking his battles.

"Okay…Is everyone ready to start the movie again?" asked Frank as he glanced around the room. "Wait, I need coffee before we start. How about you, Cate?" The children booed loudly. "Shall we brew a pot on the double before we settle down to Elsa and Anna?"

Bella and Brianne danced around the room and followed him into the kitchen singing, "The cold never bothered me anyway!"

Frank brought Cate a cup of coffee, turned the movie on again, and settled down to finish watching the film. Meanwhile, both of the girls lay together on the sectional, and Liam sat at Frank's feet on the floor.

Anyone seeing Cate would have believed she was engrossed in the film, but even though she was staring into the screen, her mind was miles away on a little girl with huge brown eyes carrying a bunny as big as she was or joyously eating an orange or proudly giving a packet of cookies to Frank and giggling while he gobbled them down or patting Hannah's white hair with affection. The more images of Kendall that came into her mind, the more she burned and boiled and nearly overflowed with anger. She had not felt like this before, and she knew if she had been in the proximity of that man, *whatever his name was,* she would have done him harm. The cell phone on the table beeped, and she almost jumped out of her chair in an effort to grab the phone and read the text from Hannah.

"What is an apnea test?"

Cate's blood ran cold. She knew that an apnea test would only be performed to check the function of the brain stem if the doctors suspected brain death. She seethed. David's death had not cut her the same way because however horrible it was, it was not intentional. Stupid? Yes. Idiotic? Of course. Careless? Absolutely. Had she forgiven yet? Not even on her best day; however, it was something she was struggling with. Just a dumb kid partying at the beach, who never dreamed his getting behind the wheel of his car that day would result in the death of another human being. The one thing it had not been was intentional. This was something altogether different, and she felt she might actually explode with the injustice and the guilt of it all. She didn't have the heart to tell Hannah the truth by text. She knew they would be informed soon enough, so she answered only "It's not good. Is Margie there?"

Seconds later, another beep. "Yes, in a conference with some doctors."

"Frank, are you free to stay with the kids for a few hours? I need to go back to the hospital."

"Of course," he answered sincerely. "Whatever you need."

She guided Liam into the kitchen. "Liam, are you comfortable spending a few hours in Frank's care. You can tell me if you aren't."

"What's going on," he asked. "I know something bad is happening. I could tell that Hannah was crying, and now you look weird too. Do we have to go back home while that crazy guy is there?"

"Absolutely not! That's never going to happen. Yes, it's true that we are upset. Someone Hannah and I care about has been hurt, and I'd like to go be with Hannah for a while. Will you be okay? I will leave you my cell number to call if you need me for any reason, but if you are uncomfortable with Frank, I understand completely, and I'll stay here. It's not a problem.

"We're okay with Frank," he assured her. "It's a kid, isn't it? Something happened to a kid you helped? Bad stuff is always happening to kids."

She knelt down, stroked his face, and promised him, "Nothing bad is going to happen to you or Bella or Brianne." She pulled him to her and gave him a big hug…and he did not resist.

"You better go," he said genuinely. "Hannah might need you. I hope the kid is okay, and Hannah too."

"Frank, I want you to buy this kid his favorite. A pizza! Any kind he wants. There's forty bucks on the island, and I'll be back in a couple of hours. I really appreciate you doing this."

"It's not a problem, Cate. We'll be just fine here. Don't worry about a thing. We'll order dinner when the movie is finished, and Liam and I will take care of everything."

"Are you leaving?" Bella questioned. "You just came home. Are you sad, Cate?"

So tiny and yet so intuitive, thought Cate as she considered the tiny upturned cherub face. "Yes, my Bella, but if you watch your movie, and Frank will order pizza for dinner, I'll be back before you go to bed so I can read you a story."

"Okay then." She reached to plant a kiss on Cate's forehead as she so often did to each of them. She turned and crawled up unto Frank's lap and rested her head on his chest, then turned her attention back to Olaf and Anna and Elsa.

Cate rose and walked to the door, shooting an appreciative glance to Liam, and was gone.

Cate arrived in the ICU twenty minutes later and found Hannah holding a crumpled sobbing Margie outside of room 3. The lights were so bright, and the unit was bustling with people dressed in blue OR scrubs, scurrying from one place to another picking up equipment, checking test results on the computer, shooting tentative glances toward Margie as if they expected her to explode and then lowering their heads again and looking in the opposite direction when she didn't.

Margie saw her first, uttering, "*She's gone. She's gone, and there's not a thing I can do about it.*" Cate helped her to a chair because she looked like she would sink right into the floor. Her knees were threatening to let her down. "I've lost my Jenny, and now my precious Kendall too. I can't think. What should I do now?" Her sobs had quieted, but this was even more disturbing.

"Where are they taking Kendall then? Are they operating?" Cate queried, knowing that was impossible but still unable to grasp the truth.

Margie answered in a whisper, "That's not Kendall anymore. She's gone to be with her mommy."

Hannah stated flatly, "They're taking her to the OR to harvest her organs for transplant so that, maybe, someone else's child can live."

They stood together behind Margie's chair, one arm encircling each other and the opposite hand resting quietly on Margie's shoulders, with the camaraderie shared in grief, watching as strangers rolled Kendall's bed away for the last time, tears streaming down their faces, and shoulders hunched in the pain of loss. There they sat in silence for an indeterminate amount of time, looking toward the doorway where Kendall had disappeared, unable to move or speak, until Cate interrupted the silence and suggested they walk down to the cafeteria for a cup of coffee. They strolled in silence down to the first floor, only to find the cafeteria closed.

"I'm so sorry." Cate gasped. "I've never been here at this hour." She looked at her watch which read 8:30 p.m. "I guess I just assumed it was always opened. There's a market across the hall that sells coffee," she suggested, but Margie murmured that all she really wanted was to go back to her hotel. She had taken a taxi in this afternoon but was now too exhausted to organize her thoughts and needed to be alone for a while. Both Cate and Hannah offered to drive her back, reluctant to leave her on her own at a time like this, but she insisted she'd call a cab, so they waited with her until it arrived to the hospital entrance.

Once Margie was safely situated inside the taxi, Hannah and Cate made their way into the parking garage. "I can meet you back at the house," Cate said to Hannah. "Or you can ride with me, and we'll get your car tomorrow."

"Don't you have to work tomorrow?" Hannah inquired. "We should take both cars."

"Oh, I had forgotten," Cate stated in exasperation. "I don't know how I'll get through the day."

She fell in behind Hannah's car and followed her home to ascertain that she made the drive in one piece. Cate couldn't bear another catastrophe at this point. Hannah parked in the driveway, and Cate pulled up out front on the street, and they slowly walked up the curved paver walkway together, arm in arm to bolster each other.

While entering the house, they were set upon by two ferocious redheaded lasses chortling with laughter, jumping and bouncing, and when Liam tried to remind them of their manners, Cate assured him this was just the medicine they needed and encouraged them in their glee to see Hannah again. They had missed her, and they weren't afraid to let her know. It eased her pain somewhat like nothing else could have done.

Cate walked into the kitchen to brew a pot of coffee, but Liam explained that Frank had shown him how to make it and that this was a fresh pot for her and Hannah. She thanked him and poured a cup for each of them and strolled back into the living room to give Hannah hers and explained to her that Liam had made it especially for them. Hannah thanked Liam profusely and asserted that she had never wanted a cup as badly as she did right now. She sat in her favorite club chair and noticed the children were bathed and in their PJs. Bella and Brianne sported cute little braided pigtails, not expertly done, which made them all the more adorable.

Cate exclaimed, "We should go up and choose your books if you want to read before bed tonight. It's getting really late."

Hannah took the girls into their room, and Cate followed Liam. Poor Frank was left to entertain himself down in the living room. Cate could hear the contagious giggling coming from the other bedroom, but in spite of that, she shared a very serious look with Liam and told him that she noticed how well he had taken care of things while she was gone.

"Did you help the girls with their baths?" He nodded in the affirmative, and she expressed to him how helpful it was to her, tonight especially, since she had been so late getting back. He shrugged and told her he was used to taking care of his sisters. It wasn't a big deal. She insisted that it was a big deal to her and thanked him for being so thoughtful. "Did you braid their hair," she asked quizzically.

She had to smile when he answered, smirking. "No, that was all Frank. He said he knew what he was doing, but he could have fooled me. It was really funny, but Bella and Brianne got a kick out of it. He's a nice man, isn't he? I think I want to be a policeman too when I grow up."

"I think you have all the qualities you'll need to make a fine policeman someday," she told him, meaning every word. "Now would you like to read the next chapter of Harry to me or to yourself?" He said he was really tired tonight and would it be okay if he skipped the reading just this once. She leaned down to kiss his forehead and pulled the cover up to his chin and wished him a goodnight.

She arrived back downstairs to find Frank and Hannah at the dining room table. Hannah had been filling Frank in on the details of the day. Cate joined them at the table but sat quietly, internalizing her feelings as she was apt to do.

Hannah sent her a worried look. "Shouldn't you turn in too? You have to work early in the morning."

Wearily shaking her head, she replied, "There's no way I could sleep. I just keep going back thinking that she was safe here. I would have been more than happy to keep her here, and the thought makes me ill."

"I think we all share that exact feeling, Cate. That's why we got into this in the first place. I'm resolved to make it work now, more than ever. We have to win this one."

Cate sighed, resigned. Hannah was right. Kendall's death couldn't be in vain. If nothing else, this was to be her battle cry, her mantra. Each time she felt like giving up, she must remember, *for Kendall.* Each time she found herself in danger of succumbing to doubt, despair or fear, *for Kendall.* There had to be purpose in this horrible, revolting, appalling situation, and she would see it through until she could comprehend. Frank rose from his chair and apologized but explained he also had to work in the morning so must take his leave, and Cate rose to walk him to the door.

"I want you to know that this breaks my heart too," he stated dejectedly. "Kendall was a tiny treasure, and I am outraged that we exposed her to harm. I don't think even Margie knew what was going on in that house."

"No," she responded, "I don't think she did. Now she has lost her daughter and granddaughter all in the same day. I can't imagine her pain. I only pray that she can overcome this loss, and Frank, I hope you know how appreciative I am of all the help you've offered and all the advice you've so generously shared. I'm keeping a tally, and I'm seriously in the red where you're concerned." He moved in close to her, but she stepped back, smiled, and offered him her hand.

He walked through the door. She closed and locked it behind him and returned to join Hannah in the dining room. "Well, my friend," she said to Hannah, "it's almost midnight. What do you want for dinner, cold pizza or chocolate ice cream?

"Chocolate ice cream of course," replied Hannah without missing a beat. "I'm famished." Cate took out the half gallon of ice cream from the freezer, grabbed two spoons from the drawer and returned to the table, handing one to Hannah.

"Salute," she said, holding her spoon aloft. Hannah clicked it in the air with her own spoon, and they both commenced glumly eating their dinner of choice. Hannah, at last, crept up to bed, but Cate strode into the living room and, while sitting in the dark, stared out the windows into the night. It was a clear cold night, and she marveled that the night sky could be so beautiful when there was such ugliness in the world. She was sitting there still when her cell phone buzzed at five in the morning.

Wondering who it could be at this hour, she glanced down at the incoming call and saw that it was her work number, so she answered right away. They were calling to offer her the day off. It was a low census day, and they had more than enough staff to cover all departments, so she could take the day off if she wanted to. How ironic she thought, not enough patients to keep everyone busy. How many more might have died last night? She accepted immediately and continued to sit quietly and stare out into the darkness.

It was Liam who found her still there when he rose at seven. He had padded down the stairs with the intention of brewing a fresh pot of coffee for Hannah and Cate. He was on his way to get the morning paper from the porch when he noticed her sitting silently in the club chair turned toward the window, so instead, he just crept in and sat by her feet with saying a word. He sensed her melancholy without even knowing why. His presence was a balm to her wounded heart, and they sat together, just that way, until they heard scampering footfalls bounding down the steps almost an hour later. At which time, they shared a smile and rose to meet the day.

"Coffee smells really good, Liam. Thanks for making it." He nodded and went to fetch the paper.

Brianne stated matter-of-factly, "We washed our face and brushed our teeth all by ourself, but there're no clothes in the drawer, so we'll just wear these today." She pointed down at her PJs.

"We'll remedy that situation after breakfast. What would you like to eat this morning?" Brianne asked for toast and jelly, and Bella asked for goldfish.

"Goldfish?" Hannah queried, descending the stairs.

"She's talking about the crackers." Liam laughed. "They're her favorite."

"I don't have any goldfish today, Bella, but I will go to the store this afternoon and pick some up. Try to think if there is anything else you need, and we'll make a list," she directed as she picked up a piece of chalk and wrote goldfish on the blackboard hanging by the fridge. "While I'm thinking of it, I should run over to the hospital safety store today and check out the car seats so we could all go."

"Have you decided not to work today?" Hannah inquired while glancing nonchalantly in Liam's direction, mouthing to him so that Cate wouldn't hear. "Did she sleep?" He shook his head in the negative in response.

"They called me off this morning around five. Apparently, there isn't enough business to keep us all occupied," she answered quietly. "I could shower and change now and go to the hospital, and we could all go the store when I get back. There's no reason to put it off until this afternoon." She ran up the stairs, and moments later, they heard the water running.

"Is she gonna be okay?" Liam asked with concern in his voice. "She was just sitting in the chair, staring out the window when I came down this morning, and I think she sat there all night long."

"She's going to be fine, Liam," Hannah assured him. "She's just sad right now. We all are, but it will be okay. Just give her a little time."

"Can we do something to help?" he asked solemnly.

"None of us can help her right now, but if I think of anything, I'll let you know. Now let's go up to the attic and find some clothes."

"The attic?" he repeated.

"Yes, sir!" Hannah answered, grinning her huge dimpled smile as she led them all the way up the stairs.

She showed them the big wooden door and the key that was inserted into the lock. Hannah explained to Liam that in these big old houses, one could lock the door from the inside or from the outside, and he fiddled with the key a bit before returning it to the lock. Liam thought it was cool, but if anyone besides Hannah or Cate had tried to get him to go into that attic, they would have had a fight on their hands. It was also creepy. As they entered into the "store," their eyes filled with amazement. Hannah showed each child how to find their size and allowed them to choose a few items for themselves. Bella just picked anything pink and girlie and needed to be reminded that it was winter. At last, she ended with pink leggings and a pretty white sweater with big ruffled pockets on the front, while Brianne found a shirt with a lovely black horse and jeans with sparkles on the pockets, and Liam chose jeans and a green-and-gold jersey. Hannah pulled socks and underwear for everyone, and they trod back down the stairs to their rooms to change.

By the time they joined up back downstairs, they realized that Cate had already gone out. Hannah made some toast and perused the fridge for the jelly, but she wanted to keep it light since she didn't know what Cate had on her mind. The kids sat around the island eating toast, drinking milk, and commenting on their new outfits. They were nearly finished when Cate walked in the garage door.

She examined the children's new clothes and complimented Hannah on her taste. She was surprised to learn the children had each chosen their own ensembles. "Well, as it turns out, we don't need car seats after all. The girls need booster seats which are already properly installed in the back seat of my car, and Liam will be okay belted as long as he's in the back. After we spiffy up the house, throw in some laundry, and make a grocery list, we can go get Bella some goldfish! Has everyone had enough to eat?"

Everyone contributed to the cleaning, even little Bella gathered all her clothes and brought them to the basket by the laundry room for washing. Beds were stripped, furniture polished. Liam used the Swiffer on the floors until they gleamed, and the bathrooms were sanitized. The kitchen and living room were tidied up, and Liam did the floors in the living room while Cate mopped the kitchen. Hannah was still upstairs tackling the laundry, but two loads were washed, and the second load was drying. She guessed there were still two or three more loads with all the sheets and towels they had used in the house. With everyone pitching in, the whole place looked good as new by lunchtime.

Cate suggested they go out for lunch and then go grocery shopping afterward, much to the delight of the kids. Liam explained that they rarely went out to eat and that he was the one feeding the girls most of the time, so they ate foods that he could prepare such as sandwiches and goldfish and broccoli and dip.

They all piled into the car. Each girl was fastened into the booster seats in the backseat, and Liam was between them, fastened into the seatbelt. Cate relinquished the driving to Hannah because she hadn't slept. They had decided on Olive Garden because the kids all liked spaghetti and because it was close to a large grocery store where they might find Bella's goldfish.

Bella and Brianne looked all around, taking in every detail as they were seated at a large table, and Cate requested a booster for Bella.

"Why do they call it a booster?" Liam asked seriously.

"Because it boosts the child up in the seat so he or she can sit at the table with adults," answered Cate. "Why do you ask?"

"My mom's boyfriend…his name is Booster. It's a stupid name. I don't know if he has any other names. Everyone just calls him Booster. I don't like the word. It makes me think of him."

"That," said Cate immediately, "is a seriously good reason to not like the word. I vote we now call these"—pointing to the little red plastic seat—"*lifters*. Who agrees?" They all laughed and raised their hands, and Liam beamed at her.

The waitress came for their orders, and all three kids wanted the chicken fingers and spaghetti, with milk to drink. Both Hannah and Cate ordered the soup and salad with water, and everyone enjoyed the breadsticks. Hannah thought, *This table can't be too difficult to wait on. We all eat practically the same things.* It was a good meal, and they genuinely relished each other's company. The mood was light, and even Cate and Hannah forgot their sadness for a little while.

CHAPTER 9

Booster

Hy-Vee was the grocery store they drove to next. The grocery list was relatively small because Cate was well supplied with staple pantry and freezer items, but she wanted the kids to be able to select a few items that they especially liked. Each girl was pushing a miniature grocery cart, and they were instructed that they could put two items into their carts. It could be whatever they liked, but they needed to really think about what they wanted since they were limited to two items each. Hannah tried to keep them to the perimeter of the store as much as possible, but she knew she would lose all control in the snack aisle when they went in search of Bella's goldfish. Brianne had a head of broccoli in her cart, but Bella, scouring every item intently, had yet to place anything in hers. Liam was following them around, enjoying watching them "shop." They were so intense, their little faces scrunched up, perusing every item very carefully. When they finally located the goldfish, Liam pointed them out to Bella, who very gingerly and daintily deposited two large bags into her cart.

"Are you sure you want two bags, Bella? That will be all for you." She grinned up at Hannah as she nodded her head, bouncing. Brianne was carefully searching the aisle up and down, and Liam asked if he could go to the next aisle over to choose a cereal. Cate gave him permission but told him to wait there for them and not go any farther. Brianne had decided she didn't want anything from this aisle, and as they were about to go round to the next one, Cate heard a loud obnoxious voice yell.

"Hey, brat! I went to jail because of you. Come here!"

Cate immediately pushed the girls in back of her toward Hannah and rounded the next aisle alone. Hannah was already heading to find some help in case it was needed.

She was just in time to witness the tall heavy rough-looking man motioning for Liam to come to him down the aisle. He was about six feet two inches and weighed about 280 pounds. His hair was dark and greasy, with some gray on the sides and bushy sideburns. His face was pockmarked as if he was a meth addict, and he wore sunglasses even though he was indoors. He was dressed in ragged, dirty jeans and a blaze-orange sweatshirt with a target emblazoned on it. Beside him stood a short thin lady with very blue eyes and matted greasy red hair. She was about five three and weighed around one hundred pounds. She also looked unwashed and unkempt and was spilling out of her clothing in various places but seemed unaware of the fact. They both appeared high or drunk or both, and she was completely indifferent to Liam or to what was happening around her. Cate couldn't decide what was wrong with them, but it was obvious that something was. She stood back for a moment to be sure of what she was witnessing and jumped when the man shouted again.

"I said, come here right now. Am I gonna have to black your other eye?"

She moved up behind Liam, laid a hand on his shoulder, and felt him relax instantly.

He whispered over his shoulder, "That is Booster...and my mom." She squeezed his shoulder to let him know she had heard him.

"This child is in my care. Are you addressing him?"

He laughed at her, leering at her in a way that made her want to cover herself. "That's Connie's brat." He motioned toward the woman at his side. "And I ended up in jail because of him," he shouted. The man's shouting was starting to draw a crowd, but he was too belligerent to notice. She turned Liam around and started to walk in the opposite direction, but Booster wouldn't have that. He made several large fast intimidating strides toward her, yelling, "Stop right there! I'm still talking to that little bastard!"

That did it! Cate maneuvered Liam behind her and turned on Booster, making several long strides of her own so that he was backed up a few steps in his surprise. She was already furious over events that had nothing to do with him, but he couldn't know that, and these circumstances were similar enough to make her blood boil.

"Are you seriously telling me that a big guy like you has nothing better to with his day than to bully an eight-year-old boy in the middle of a crowded grocery store? I don't care whose child he is. Today, he's in my care, and I won't allow you to badger him!"

There was applause from the group of people that had crowded around him to watch and then, and only then, did he take notice of how many people were witnessing this exchange. She was aware that she had embarrassed him. The color rose in his face, and Cate recognized that she had shamed him and, thus, made a powerful enemy. He turned and left the store, but she felt sure she had not seen the last of Booster. She looked around and saw that several patrons and employees had moved in to assist her had she needed it, and she felt grateful. But crazy as it was, she felt no fear. She only felt the seething, boiling anger that seemed to be a part of her now. She knelt down and searched Liam's face.

"Are you okay?" He was grinning from ear to ear.

"Never been better" was his reply. He walked over to the Cheerios and picked the box up and placed it into Hannah's cart, still smiling.

Cate looked into Brianne's cart and asked her if she had any idea of what her second item would be and could only smirk when she was told that, of course, it would be dip for her trees. The little family ambled to the back of the store to the dairy aisle in order for Brianne to choose some dip to place in her cart. On the way to the front, they walked through the ice cream section, and no one was tempted until Bella set her eyes on the multicolored popsicles and stopped in her tracks. She glanced into her cart and back again to the popsicles so often but just couldn't make up her mind. Finally, Liam whispered into Hannah's ear, and she nodded her head in agreement.

Liam picked up the popsicles and placed them in the cart as he said to Bella, "I only have cereal. I'll get these popsicles as my second pick and share them with you."

Bella reached up, relieved that she no longer had to decide, and gave him a big hug. They checked out and wandered over to the car, unpacked the grocery items into the back of the Escape, and took their seats. Cate made sure everyone was safely buckled in and made her way back to the passenger seat, feeling grateful that Hannah was driving. She was finally getting tired, and the thought of her soft bed was sounding pretty good about now. Nobody noticed the green-and-white pickup that followed them out of the parking lot. They had the radio turned up, and Hannah was singing, making the kids giggle. Everyone was having a good time, but nobody noticed the pickup following them into Middleton. When they pulled into the driveway of 222 Bristol Street, nobody saw the pickup truck that cruised slowly past and continued on down the street.

They unloaded the groceries and entered into the garage door through the kitchen. Hannah gave Bella her goldfish and asked her to take a few but to place the bags in the pantry on a shelf that she could reach, and she toddled off to do as she was instructed. Hannah thought that she might break the bags down into snack-sized bags later so that Bella could grab a small bag at a time when she wished.

She washed her hands in order to cut Brianne's broccoli down into small pieces and placed them into snack bags in the fridge. She first washed it and pulled out a cutting board and proceeded to chop. In no time, she had filled ten little snack bags. Hannah lined them up in a Tupperware tray that could be placed on a low shelf in the fridge, but seeing plenty of room still in the tray, she decided to break down some of Bella's crackers the same way. She entered the pantry and saw the two bags of goldfish perched on a low shelf, neither was opened. She took one bag into the kitchen and placed a small handful of crackers into ten separate bags, just like she had done for Brianne. She then placed them side by side in the tray and called the girls into the kitchen to see what she had done.

"We will keep this tray on the bottom shelf so you can reach them when you want them," she explained. They looked up at her and bounced excitedly. She allowed them to place the tray on the lower shelf and close the door.

Cate had apologized and excused herself to go take a nap. She was too tired to run on anger anymore today. Hannah and Liam were both relieved that she finally went to lay down for a while. They were worried about her. She sent the girls up to nap as well and asked Liam to lay in his room and rest or read as he wished. When everyone was resting, she took the time to call the motel where Margie said she'd be staying to check on her, only to find that she had checked out around seven in the morning, with no plan to return. She thanked the clerk and hung up. That was curious. Hannah thought she was staying in town to make memorial arrangements. Maybe it was just too much for her to face. She found herself wishing there had been more she could have done, but even though the poor woman was beside herself with grief, she wouldn't allow them to help, not even to drive her to the motel.

She realized that someone was knocking on the door and strode over to answer it. Frank was looking through the glass, and as she opened the door to allow him in, neither of them saw the green pickup parked across the street drive away. Frank stepped inside and asked how Hannah was doing.

"I'm coping," she responded. "How are you handling everything?"

"I'm the same as you," he answered. "I'm about as ticked off as I've ever been and not sure how to handle it yet. Is Cate in? I've come by to tell her about an idea Nobie had to show the kids around the fire station."

"That's a terrific idea," Hannah said. "Thank him for us and tell him to call, and we'll set something up. The kids would love that experience. Cate is resting right now. She sat up fuming all night, and she didn't lie down at all until about twenty minutes ago. I hope she'll sleep for a while, but there is something I need to share with you." He raised a quizzical brow and invited her to speak. She poured him a cup of coffee and related the whole story of what happened in the grocery store. "It was frightening," Hannah explained, "but Cate wasn't scared at all. She stood up to him, and he backed down. He looked like a nasty character, and the *mother*! Never spoke a word to any of her children, and she hasn't seen them for days. Maybe she was too out of it to see them at all. She wasn't in good shape."

"Do you know his name or what he looked like?"

"Liam knew his name. He said everyone calls him Booster. We made a big joke of calling the booster seats lifts from now on because he commented that he doesn't like the word booster."

Frank nodded his head. "Oh yeah," he said. "I know who he is, and he is a nasty character. He's called Booster because that's how he supports his drug habit. He steals or "boosts" electronics from homes and stores and sells or pawns the items for cash. His real name is Victor Whitehead. He didn't grow up around here. He relocated from Milwaukee or Chicago…I can't recall. We have arrested him a couple of times. Possession and assault, I think. Tell Cate to steer clear of him. He's big, mean and, because of his drug use, has killed off most of his brain cells. He's stupid too. It's a very dangerous combination."

"Don't worry about that. I think she received that signal loud and clear. I was interested in the mother, Connie. How does a woman bear three children and expose them to people like Booster?"

"Connie is another story altogether. My guess is, in her experience, there are no other kinds of people. That's all she's ever known. She grew up with a hard-drinking father. The mother died early on and left a bunch of kids in his care, three or maybe four. Connie was the oldest, so she probably got the worst of that deal, but all of those kids left as soon as they were able and moved far away from here. Heaven only knows what went on inside those walls. She's had a drug problem for a few years, which is why DCF has been involved. There was a sister that used to take them in occasionally, but she's been out of the picture for months, and I'm not sure what happened to her. Connie's only about twenty-two, but you wouldn't know it looking at her. She's had a rough time of it. Pregnant before she was even able to start high school, so she never moved past the eighth grade."

Hannah took a few minutes to digest the information she was given. *Another one of life's lessons*, she thought. This was one she had trouble learning, so it kept cropping up in her life to remind her to never judge other people since you can't know what kind of private hell they may be living. She'd leave the judging to someone else and do whatever she could to help.

"Hannah, I know I'm being a crazy cop, and I don't want to frighten you, but answer a few questions for me will ya?" She nodded her assent and waited for him to continue. "Do you keep your phone on your person?"

"No, but it's close by. It's in my purse," she answered, and she felt as if her heart rate was increasing.

"Go get it for me. Program my cell number into it and keep it on you at all times. Put it in your pocket."

She walked across the room to retrieve her purse and pulled out the phone. "What's the number?" she asked solemnly and typed it in as he relayed it. "I gotta tell ya Frank, you are alarming me a little bit."

"I don't want you to be alarmed," he stated. "I want you to be prepared. Think of Jenny Martin at the bottom of her stairs. If she'd had her phone, she wouldn't have been lying in that basement for over twenty hours. Just get used to having it with you at all times. If your pockets are too small…its winter, choose a sweater with pockets or a sweatshirt with a pouch. They even make arm bands that you can Velcro on that hold your phone. Now call me. Let's make sure the number is in properly." She dialed, and his pocket rang. "See, on me at all times." He smiled. "I was a boy scout."

He was moving toward the door but called over his shoulder, "Don't forget Nobie will be calling about the tour of the firehouse and tell Cate to program in my number and to keep her phone within reach. Appease the cop in me and come lock the door behind me." He stood on the porch for a few minutes unbeknownst to Hannah and perused the neighborhood but saw nothing suspicious. He walked to first one neighbor, then another, and held a short conversation with the homeowners, until he had spoken with everyone in proximity to 222 Bristol Street. At last, he crawled into his unmarked police car and was on his way back to the station.

Hannah had taken a chicken out of the freezer and dropped it into a brine early this morning and now started to prepare it for roasting. She dried it carefully and seasoned the inside and outside of the bird. Next, she smeared a butter-and-herb mixture under the skin over the breast meat and filled the cavity with aromatics and lemon and placed it breast side up in a roasting pan. She surrounded it with root vegetables and sprinkled a little seasoning over them, and topped it all off with fresh thyme. If she slow roasted it for forty-five minutes to an hour she would have a complete meal, and she would only need to prepare a salad and butter some rolls for dinner.

The children crept down the stairs but livened up when they saw that Hannah was in the kitchen. Bella pranced and twirled her way right to the refrigerator, opened the door, and scooped out one of her bags of goldfish, smiling up at Hannah as if trying to charm her into winning her approval regarding the snack. The look was priceless, and her antics worked. Hannah could only smile. In only a few days, she could observe that they were all blossoming in this environment, and she liked thinking that some of it had to do with her and Cate. It warmed her heart and made her feel incredibly lucky that she was able to contribute to this endeavor.

Dinner was working on its own and starting to smell delicious, and she was trying to think of a way to entertain them for about a half hour.

"Do you know how to play Old Maid?" she asked them, and she looked around at each in turn as they shook their heads no. "Great. I'm going to show you what we used to do long before cell phones and computers were around." She rummaged through a drawer in the kitchen until she found a deck of playing cards. She instructed them to all take a place around the island as she searched through the cards and removed all the queens except the queen of clubs. Liam helped the girls up into the barstools.

"Have you ever seen a deck of cards before?" she asked, and they answered that they had not.

Holding the queen of clubs up so they could all see the card, she explained that the person holding this card at the end of the game would be dubbed the Old Maid. The kids looked at each other and giggled in anticipation. She further explained that each card, except the old maid card, had a sister, and that they looked just alike except the color. Holding up two aces, she showed them. Now the object of the game was to match each card with its sister card until there was only the old maid card left.

"Shall we play a practice game to make sure everyone understands?" The kids all shouted yes! She dealt all the cards out and instructed, "Without showing everyone else your cards, you first want to match all the cards in your hand that have sisters and place them in front of you facedown on the table. These are called pairs... like a pair of socks." Searching her hand, she located all her pairs and laid them in front of her, then waited until the others had done the same. "It's hard at first because there are so many cards to hold on to, but it gets easier when there are fewer cards in your hand."

Liam was finished and waited patiently for his sisters. Bella had a little trouble because her hands were so tiny, but she managed and had concocted her own system by checking a few cards at a time. When asked if she wanted help, she stated emphatically that she could do it by herself. At last, everyone was ready to move on to the next step.

"Okay, now each person draws a card from the person seated on their right like this." She held her hand of remaining cards out facedown toward Liam and asked him to pick one. He chose one, looked at it and laughed, and placed a pair facedown on the table. "Okay," Hannah said. "Next, you offer your hand to Brianne."

So he turned toward his sister and held his cards facedown to her. She chose one, found its pair, and placed it facedown in front of her, then proudly turned to Bella and repeated the gesture without being told. Bella chose a card and scrunched up her face as she concentrated on the task before her but laid down her pair too. Then she offered her hand to Hannah and giggled as Hannah chose the old maid card.

Hannah thought, *Oh, yes! She's got the hang of this already.* They continued around the table, but Liam never chose the old maid card, so in the end, she held up the card and declared, "I'm the old maid!

"Let's play again," squeaked Bella. "That was so much fun!" And Brianne joined in clapping.

"We'll play after dinner, or you can take the cards into the dining room and play together if you want." They gathered up the cards and moved to the dining room to entertain themselves while Hannah finished dinner.

Cate entered the kitchen and inquired about the aroma that was now filling the whole house with goodness.

"The way I figure it, you've only had about four hours of sleep. Do you feel rested?" quizzed Hannah.

"I feel like a bear awaking from hibernation, groggy and thick and starving," she said, sniffing the air. "What is that tantalizing smell? It woke me from a sound sleep. Oh, by the way, I folded the clothes in the dryer and started another load. The kids now have a few clean things in their dressers."

"Roast chicken, and it's probably done. I'll take it out and let it sit on the cutting board for a few minutes. That'll give me time to throw a salad together and grab some bread. Would you ask the kids to pick up the cards and help set the table, please?"

The kids picked up while Hannah placed the plates on the table. Brianne brought in the silver, and Bella grabbed the napkins. Liam was filling water glasses and delivered them two at a time to the table. By the time Hannah had finished, the table was in order.

Bella was in the middle of explaining the art of Old Maid to Cate when the phone rang, and Hannah excused herself to answer it.

"Oh, hello, Nobie." She smiled at Cate, signaling that she knew what it was about. "Frank told me…yes! It's a wonderful idea, and we really appreciate you thinking of us. Well, we're right in the middle of dinner, but would you mind calling in an hour so we can work out the details? Yes, and thank you again." She hung up the phone and turned to see all four faces curiously staring at her and grinning, as if they could extract information from her with their eyes. "Stop it. You're acting creepy." And she laughed at them.

When she sat back down, she informed them that Nobie had offered to host them at the fire station tomorrow and give them a tour of the station and the truck, if they were interested. School starts back again on Tuesday, and there won't be another chance until Christmas break. They were all very excited by the invitation, and the little ones had trouble concentrating on their dinner. Hannah mentioned the visit from Frank as well and suggested that Cate add his cell number into her own phone, but Cate assured her she had it already.

"He also wants us to start keeping the phones in our pockets as opposed to leaving them on the table or in our purses. He says it's just smart to be prepared all the time, and when you think about it, it does make sense."

Cate thanked Hannah for the delicious meal, and they all agreed the chicken was the superb. The phone rang just as they were loading the dishwasher.

Cate called out, "I'm going to take that in the office…It's probably Nobie."

And she hurried into the office to catch it before it rang again. She was making plans to bring the kids to the fire station at around ten on the following morning when she was distracted by something outside. The office was dark, and she hadn't bothered to turn on the light as she entered because she was running to answer the phone. Curious about what exactly had distracted her, she leaned closer to the window and peered out. She saw a green-and-white pickup parked across the street, about ten feet down from the streetlight. The thing that had attracted her attention was a lighter being struck in the cab of the truck.

"That's odd," she whispered to herself as she began to watch the figure in the truck. It couldn't be more than 15 degrees outside today. Why would anyone be sitting out in a cold truck in the dark? The vehicle wasn't running. She looked for a plate number but could only make out DFN as her angle from the window obscured the numbers. "Nobie…will you do me a favor? This may be nothing, but there is a green-and-white pickup parked across from my house, plate starts with DFN. Someone is sitting over there in the dark scoping out this house. Could you call Frank and tell him? Maybe he can check the tags and call me back to tell me I'm crazy? It's just odd, and it's creeping me out since I have the children in the house."

"I'll call him right now. Keep your phone handy."

Cate wished she could get a better look. She didn't want to frighten the children, but she was getting a prickly feeling that put her on edge. Frank was right. Where had she put her cell phone? She thought it was on the table in the living room, so she slowly stepped in that direction and saw it lying on the table by her chair. She was still enveloped in darkness, but a bit of light was spilling into the room from the dining area, and for some reason she couldn't have explained, she didn't want to be seen from the street. The kids were trying to talk Hannah into another game of cards, and she could hear them laughing and talking happily in the distance. Her senses were heightened, and it felt as if time were passing in slow motion, and as she reached the phone, the door of the pickup swung open and out stepped a figure Cate had no difficultly identifying. She'd have known him anywhere—it was Booster, and he was coming in this direction.

"Hannah! Listen carefully right now! Take the children to the attic and lock yourselves in from the inside. Got it? Take the key inside and lock the door. Call 911 once you're safely inside and don't come out until I come to get you! You have your phone on you, right?"

Everything stopped in the dining room, and Hannah instantly gathered up the children and rushed them up the stairs, half carrying little Bella. All the way to the top they climbed, and she pushed them inside as she grabbed the key from the lock and pulled the door closed behind her—but she couldn't do it! She wasted precious seconds trying to decide. She had no idea what was happening, but she didn't doubt for a moment the urgency in Cate's voice. Whatever it was, she couldn't leave Cate to face it alone, and if she were locked on the other side of this door, she'd be no help whatsoever. Decision made, she knelt down and spoke directly to Liam.

"You know how to lock this door, don't you?" As he stoically nodded the affirmative, she spoke fervently, "I would like to go inside with you, but Cate might need my help. Your job is to stay inside that door. Take my phone and call 911, then call Frank. Do not come out for any reason until someone you trust comes to get you. Keep your sisters back away from the door and wait. Remember, do not open the door for anyone except someone you trust no matter what happens. Got it?"

His eyes were as huge as saucers, but he nodded and said, "I got it!"

He stepped inside, and Hannah heard the clicking noise that assured her that the door was locked. She checked it anyway. She was debating going back down the stairs when she heard a crash of breaking glass and backed up into the darkness to listen.

"Come here, little chickies. Come to papa," he cackled.

Hannah recognized the voice from the grocery store immediately and now understood the urgency. She didn't want to endanger Cate so she stood stock still in the darkness and listened carefully to his ranting. He apparently didn't see Cate anywhere as he rambled from room to room, searching for the inhabitants of this house. He knew they were here somewhere, so he took his time searching and kept calling out "chickie, chickie come out…come to papa" from room to room as he kept up his slow careful pursuit. He must be out of his mind. Did he think he could get away with this? Hannah had to think fast. She didn't want to be caught on this landing with nowhere to go, so she eased herself carefully and quietly down to the second level and considered her choices of where best to hide. She slid into the laundry closet and, as gingerly as she could, crept down on the other side of the washer and waited. She could hear both floors from this vantage point and a cursory glance of the closet wouldn't reveal the space she was hiding in. It was deceptive and, she hoped, would work to her advantage. If he did see her though, she was screwed as she wouldn't be able to maneuver out of this tight space quickly enough to avoid him. She waited and listened. He was getting frustrated, and he was getting louder.

"Come on out now! I ain't got all day!"

There was a crash of glass breaking, of furniture being tossed around. *Was that the Christmas tree? So…he was in the living room*, she thought. Next, she heard what sounded like dishes being thrown into the dining room. Crash! Crash! Crash! Now the kitchen…she heard footfalls on the stairs…but it sounded as if he were bouncing off the walls, banging first into one wall and then to the other side. *Good,* she thought. *Maybe he'll fall and break his neck!* He can't have been sober, but she had no idea what kind of high he was on. She heard him enter one room and then another, taking time to check closets and under beds. He spent more time in Cate's room, and Hannah realized she was glad that she couldn't see what he was doing in there. He started to mumble under his breath, but she could hear him all too well from where she was hiding.

"Where the hell are they hiding? Damn bitch must have seen me coming."

He threw something into the door of the laundry room, and it crashed and broke on the floor outside the door. She drew in a sharp breath of dread, thinking he might actually see her from this angle, but instead, it turned into a benefit when the weight of it pushed the bifold door on the washer side closed and offered her more cover. He peered in but didn't notice the space on the opposite side of the washing machine. He continued on down the hall to the extra bedroom, where upon finding nothing, started, by the sound of it, tearing the bed apart and throwing the pieces around. He made his way to the landing and noticed upon closer inspection in the darkness that the stairway continued higher up.

"Oh yeah! Hiding in the attic, chicky chicky," he screamed up into the darkness.

Hannah was glad she had chosen to move, or she would have been trapped on the landing right where he was approaching. He reached the heavy wooden door and tried to open it and, when he found it locked, began to scream through the door.

"Do ya think a little door is gonna stop me! I found ya, didn't I? Open the door! OPEN the DOOR, or I'm gonna break it apart!"

Hannah heard a small voice yell, "No! Go away, Booster!"

"Ah, don't be like that, honey!" he screeched. "I just want your brother to come out!"

There wasn't another response, but he had gotten what he wanted—confirmation that they were all hiding in the attic. He tried to wrestle with the heavy door again but had to admit that he was getting nowhere, so he retraced his steps and wound up in the kid's bathroom. Hannah thought he might be peeing all over the room.

He was hooting and babbling to himself as he came back to the landing and descended the stairs back to the first level. Where were the cops? Where was Frank? She strained to listen, but he was farther away now, and it was more difficult to distinguish his movements. He could have been in the fridge. She waited for what seemed like an eternity.

Cate had shoved herself into the broom closet in the pantry. A cursory glance into the little storage space wouldn't reveal the closet. One had to be looking for it to see it. Gabe had designed the cabinetry specifically for the purpose of hiding the extra storage from view, simply for the aesthetics of the space. After she heard the door open and close, she eased herself to the door to listen. He traveled upstairs and back again. She could see that he was aggravated and thought for a moment he was coming back into the pantry and readied herself to sprint back to the closet, but he opened the garage door instead. She was uncomfortable knowing he was rambling through the garage. She owned all sorts of tools, and they were all stored in the garage cupboards. Trying to peer through the tiny opening in the door was difficult, but she managed to watch him return with her can of turpentine and a rag, and she could only conceive of one reason he might be interested in that particular item—fire. She knew she had no choice but to distract him, and the only way she could accomplish that was to reveal herself.

Hannah's legs were starting to cramp up, and she wasn't sure how much longer she could stay in this position, when she thought she heard voices. What was that? WHAT WAS THAT? She definitely heard more than one voice. Her hope retreated from her when she recognized that other voice was Cate's. She had to get out of this space! She eased herself up onto the washer as quietly as possible, maneuvered herself out of the laundry room, and tiptoed down the hall to the landing. Whatever else happened, she was glad to be out of that tight space.

Listening from the top of the stairs, she could hear them. It sounded to Hannah like Cate was negotiating. She could hear their voices coming from the direction of the office and could make out that he was asking about her valuables. Threatening her—no—

threatening the children. He was threatening to burn the attic if she didn't give him what he wanted. She eased over toward the door and glanced in to where they stood. Cate had led him into the office on the pretext of retrieving her purse. Hannah listened as she heard Cate offer to take him to her bank or to an ATM. She was trying to convince him to leave the house, trying to lure him away from the children. That's the moment when Hannah saw it, and she understood his intent. He was holding the can of turpentine and a rag that Cate had used when she was ready to refinish the dining room table. It must have come from the garage. Cate must have been able to see him from wherever she was hiding, and when he had emerged from the garage with the turpentine, she must have come out of hiding to distract him. She had put herself in danger to protect those children from fire. What in the world was wrong with people these days!

Rage churned up in Hannah. The same rage that had threatened to engulf Cate a few days earlier. In her mind's eye, she saw Gabe laboring over every detail in this house. She saw Cate painting and cleaning until she was exhausted but still smiling. She saw Kendall sitting at the island with her bunny in her arms and Liam lying on the floor of the doorway to the girl's room, and *she knew no fear*. She crept into the dining room searching for a weapon and, seeing none, continued on into the kitchen, glancing quickly around the room. Then she spotted it. Standing beside the stove in a cobalt blue Fiesta ware crock protruded a multitude of kitchen utensils of every kind, and she chose what she felt to be the most appropriate weapon at her disposal—a huge heavy solid-wood baker's rolling pin—and she calmly walked into the living room, knowing she intended to cause some damage. She never even paused, and when she entered stealthily behind him, she could see he had his hands around Cate's throat and was lifting her entirely off the floor and practically spitting into her face.

"You ain't such a smart ass now, are ya!"

He sneered as he watched her face turn red, and her eyes began to bulge. She was kicking and trying to pry his filthy fingers from her throat, but he was so confident that he never heard Hannah walk up behind him and swing her rolling pin with all her might against the back of his head. He dropped to his knees like a loser in a boxing match and ended facedown on the floor.

Cate dropped to the floor as well and began rubbing her throat and gasping for breath but still managed to whisper, "You are supposed to be locked behind that big wooden door in the attic. What are you doing down here?"

"It's a good thing I'm not, sassy pants! You'd still be hanging in midair in the office. Are you okay, by the way? You *had* to tick him off, didn't you? Are you able to move? Can you go unlock the door for the police? I'm going to stay here in case he decides to get up again. I've seen too many of *those* movies."

Cate laughed at her friend and managed to rise from the floor to go open the door. She came back toward Hannah bowing jokingly.

"I am in awe of you! You honestly saved my life tonight."

Cate took the car keys from a hook in the entryway and pressed the car alarm button. It screamed through the neighborhood, and it didn't take long for neighbors to start coming out and question what all the commotion was about. Several people were hurrying toward their house. There were so many people outside that it seemed at least one person from every house was coming to check on them.

Blaring sirens could now be heard, and cars with lights flashing pulled up into the drive and parked in the street. Frank came running into the house and inspected each of them to make sure there were no injuries.

"Are the kids all okay?" he asked, and he was assured they were fine.

Cate told him that when Booster was out of her house, she would liberate the kids from the attic, but not until. He then turned his attention to the intruder. He called for an ambulance when he saw the blood on the floor and recognized that it was coming from a head wound. He looked up at Cate, but she shrugged and said, "Don't look at me. I was otherwise occupied."

Then he turned in exasperation toward Hannah, and with his brow raised in inquiry, he asked, "Seriously? You did this? I've known you all my life, and I've never seen you lose your temper."

Hannah looked Frank directly in the eye and spouted, "I wish I could tell you that I'm sorry, but I'm not. As a matter-of-fact, I'm half tempted to hit him again. He nearly killed Cate, and he threatened to burn down Gabe's beautiful masterpiece, with the children in it. I'm not even a little bit sorry. He had no right to come in here and threaten this family."

Cate threw her arms around Hannah's shoulder and led her to the dining room table to sit down. "We need to sit down, drink coffee, locate something to eat, and contemplate the happenings of the day."

"Hey," called Hannah, "does anyone here know how to work a coffeepot? I can't possible manage anything that complicated right now."

The ambulance had come and gone within twenty minutes, and two officers followed it to the hospital. Neighbors were milling around outside, some trying to be useful, others just curious onlookers, but because this was a crime scene, they were being kept to the perimeter of the property. Hannah climbed the stairs to extricate the children from the attic and to let them know that all was well. She could only imagine how frightening this was for them. Officers were walking through the house cataloging the damage. Frank was taking a statement from Cate of the events as they occurred. Bella was appalled by the mess strewn all around them and asked Hannah severely who had made it. Brianne looked at all the damage surrounding them, and tears fell silently down her face.

Cate saw their distress and wished she could do something to prevent it. Instead, she gathered both girls close to her and whispered to Brianne very seriously, "What is this?"

Brianne looked at all of the destruction and then back to Cate again and answered very solemnly, "Stuff."

"That's exactly right, kiddo! This is all just stuff and can be cleaned up in no time. You and your brother and sister are safe. Hannah is safe and so am I...so I think we're all pretty lucky. How did you like your stay in the attic? I hope it wasn't too scary for you. You have all been very brave tonight."

"I was brave," she responded. "I told Booster to go away. Liam told me I should be quiet though, so I did. Liam called the policeman for us."

"I think I'm in need of some coffee. Does anyone else want a drink or a snack? Hannah, do you need something?" She had busied herself sweeping up glass from the kitchen and dining room.

The police had taken photos of all the damage, and some of them had returned to the station, but Frank and a few others were still around, and someone was going through the pickup out on the street. They were also still monitoring the outside of the property since Cate reported that was where she had noticed him approaching the house. Cate felt very grateful no one was hurt, but as she scanned the damage, she did feel a little bit sick. There was so much destruction, and for what purpose? She and Hannah decided to order pizza for the kids, mainly so they wouldn't have to prepare a meal in this mess. There would be no cooking in this house for a few days at least. Priority would be to clean up the bathrooms and bedrooms so the kids could bathe and sleep tonight. They decided to order extra for the officers and neighbors still hanging around outside in the cold.

She asked Frank if she could ask some of the neighbors in to thank them for trying to help and to allow them to warm themselves by the fire. He said crime scene techs were finished, so it would be permissible to let them in. She switched the fire on, and she stepped out into the cold and introduced herself to several of the neighbors. She invited them in for coffee and pizza. She noticed a couple of people she had met before. She'd met Jack and his wife when she and Hannah had been out walking in the conservatory, and Steve helped her at the hardware store when she was buying supplies. She didn't even know they were her neighbors, and she told herself that needed to be remedied. She'd make a better effort to get to know these people.

"I hope you'll understand that we had a situation here today, and the place has been trashed, so try to excuse the war zone."

After examining the window that Booster had smashed, Steve remarked that he had some plywood in his garage that would work as a temporary fix and left to go fetch it.

Nobie and Karen arrived, and when they came through the door, they were already asking what they could do to help. Nobie explained that after talking with Cate, he had expected to hear back from either her or Frank, and when he didn't, he decided to come over to see what the problem was.

"Karen was at my place, and she wanted to come too." As he took in the wreckage, he said, "I think what you need here is a cleanup crew. It's not as bad as it appears at first sight. Show us where you keep the cleaning supplies, mops and brooms and such, and we'll split up and tackle the mess one room at a time. If we all pitch in, it'll be done in no time at all."

They split themselves up into teams and set to work. Nobie was right. Most of the mess was actually broken glass. Some lamps had been broken, a big window, and lots of dishes, including some of Cate's Fiesta ware that had been displayed on the open shelving. The pizza arrived, and Hannah laid out a spread on the island for anyone that wanted a snack while they worked. Even a couple of the officers were trying to piece the Christmas tree back together again. Karen was on laundry duty and washed everything in sight just to be sure all traces of *him* were gone. The kid's bathroom was the worst, but it soon sparkled like new and had an array of clean towels stacked up, enough for bath time for the kids. She asked Liam if he would see to getting the girls ready for their baths and into PJs, which he agreed to.

"After you're all ready for bed, come downstairs, and we'll try to have everything cleaned up by the time you come back down."

Liam rounded the girls up and climbed the stairs to start the bath water. He was really tired and was actually looking forward to bedtime. Although he would never admit it, he had been pretty scared waiting in the attic. Not knowing what was wrong was bad enough, but then when he heard Booster's voice at the door, he'd been so scared that something bad had happened to Cate and Hannah. It seemed like forever waiting and waiting, trying to keep Bella and Brianne from being frightened. He knew how bad Booster could be, and he had almost expected that he would get that door open and then there would be hell to pay. All he really wanted now was a bath and bed. He felt pretty darn lucky that everything was okay now. He felt like trouble followed him wherever he went, and he wondered what it would be like to have a normal life like other kids. Booster came and wrecked Cate's house because of him.

Cate and Hannah were thanking everyone for all their help, and it was only then that they were informed that Frank had asked the neighborhood to keep an eye on her house. He had informed all the neighbors that a little extra diligence would be appreciated because he believed a threat existed. Steve had managed to board up the broken window, and hearing the conversation, he apologized. He said he was really sorry that someone was able to enter the house without him noticing.

"It gets dark so early now, and he must have purposely waited to cover his movements. What a creep."

Cate strolled over to Nobie, and Karen and engaged them in conversation. "Don't think for a minute that I'm going to let you leave without a detailed account of how the two of you ended up being at Nobie's house together when I spoke to him. How long has this been blossoming?" she asked, grinning.

"We hadn't met before your Thanksgiving Day dinner," Nobie replied, reaching for Karen and pulling her close to him. "I don't know how we missed each other, living in a small town and working in such close proximity to one another, but technically, we have you and Hannah to thank for the introduction."

Karen gushed, smiling brightly. "He is so smart, thoughtful, and funny that I couldn't resist him. Not to mention how good he is to look at. We've been together every day since Thanksgiving."

Hannah suggested that they organize a block party in the spring or summer to get to know all the neighbors and that, maybe, they should organize some kind of neighborhood watch as well. Several of them declared that it was a great idea and promised to bring it up when the weather was a little warmer so plans could be made.

The kids were all freshly scrubbed and decked out in PJs when they came back downstairs. Cate told them about Nobie's invitation to tour the firehouse and asked if they would be up to it tomorrow. Liam smiled and nodded, but Cate thought his heart wasn't in it. The girls, on the other hand, were very excited, and they performed their little bounce, much to the delight of everyone in the room. Cate said that if they wanted, they could have a half hour of TV instead of a book tonight, and being so tired, they all thought it would be nice to just be entertained for a little while.

As the kids engrossed themselves in television, the adults were saying goodnight. Cate was very grateful for all the help cleaning up, and she felt indebted to Steve for making sure the window was safe and secure for tonight, not to mention keeping the cold out. All the guests had returned to their own homes, promising to check back to make sure she didn't need anything. The officers returned to work, and all that remained was her little family. When Cate looked around at them, she noted that each of the children was losing the battle with the sandman and urged them to head up to bed. They came over to her for their usual peck on the forehead and scampered off without a word of protest.

"Are you staying here or going home tonight? You have to open in the morning, don't you?" Cate inquired.

"No, I have one more blissful day with you, guys. Michael and Grace are handling tomorrow. Are you taking the kids to the firehouse in the morning?

"Yes," she replied. "I think we should return to normalcy posthaste. It would be better for them, don't you think?"

"I agree. I'm concerned about Liam. He may only need time, but he was very quiet. Not himself. Maybe you could talk to him tomorrow and make sure he's handling this whole situation. He looked like he had the weight of the whole world on his shoulders."

"Okay sure. I'll have a chat with him in the morning. He has been under so much pressure, and I don't doubt that Booster showing up here brought back some bad memories. He has been taking care of his sisters for so long on his own. I also wonder what effect this will have on his mother. I guess we'll know soon enough. Let's turn in. I'm longing for my pillow, and we have a date with Nobie in the morning."

CHAPTER 10

The Man-Child and Protector

The kids were up before either Cate or Hannah and got themselves dressed quietly and tramped down the stairs. Liam made some sandwiches and threw them and a few pieces of fruit in a bag and then after making sure they were bundled up to buffer them from the cold, he herded the girls silently out the door and into the subzero morning air. Fortunately, Cate had awakened and was relishing the morning sun shining in from her window when she spied the tiny little trio moving down the street, one behind the other like a miniature winter parade. She threw on her slippers and a robe and flew down the stairs and out the door, calling to them, half bounding half sliding on the icy sidewalk, trying to catch up to them without breaking her neck.

"Liam, where are you going," she shouted after them. "Come back. We need to talk. Come back inside and tell me what's on your mind. Have I done something to hurt you?"

He turned to face her and looked so dejected she couldn't believe she hadn't recognized his pain earlier.

"We can't stay anymore. He came because of us. He almost hurt you, and he tore up your house. Trouble follows us everywhere. It's my fault".

"What? Booster is your fault? That's not true," she asserted. "You aren't responsible for his actions. He's a horrible man that likes to cause other people pain, but he's not going to hurt us anymore. Come back inside and let's talk about it before you decide. I'm gonna freeze out here. Come back inside. I'll whip up some French toast, and you can tell me what's on your mind, then if you still want to leave, I'll drive you wherever you want to go."

He wore such a look of determination that Cate was afraid she'd never convince him to return to the house. His shoulders slumped, and he held his head low, but he turned and started back up the sidewalk with his sisters in tow. Slowly trudging back toward the warmth of the house, they resembled Russian nesting dolls, rounded from bundles of winter ware and decreasing in size from one to another, faces bright pink from the cold.

Hannah was in the kitchen, flitting from fridge to stove in an effort to decide on a breakfast menu when the frigid quartet blew in from the cold.

"What shall it be?" she asked in an attempt to ignore the obvious.

"I have promised French toast. Will that suit you?" stated Cate sedately. "And some hot tea or cocoa would be nice. I'll make myself a cup of coffee to warm these icicles I call hands. Could you entertain the girls while Liam and I have a little chat?"

"Of course! We'll be fine in here, won't we, girls?" she responded. "Why don't you go sit by the fire? You can warm up and talk at the same time."

"Excellent notion," Cate replied as she led Liam out into the living room. "Will you bring Liam a cup of something to warm his bones when it's ready?" Hannah said that she would. "Okay, kiddo. Tell me what's on your mind. Why do you want to leave? Because I sure do love having you guys around to class up the place."

"I don't know how to explain it," he countered.

"Just start from the beginning. We've got all day, and if I understand how you feel, maybe I can help. It's really hard to make all of life's decisions alone. We all need other people in our lives that we trust to lighten the load we carry every day, and Liam, your load is much too heavy for an eight-year-old boy. It's sort of like cleaning up the mess Booster made of this house. It was done in hours with the help of all those neighbors and friends, but if I had to do it alone, it would still be a disaster, and I would feel totally overwhelmed."

"I worry about my sisters, and I want them to be safe," he began. "At the same time, I don't want our problems to bother you or Hannah. Living with my mom wasn't so bad at first, but she never had enough money for things like food and clothes. When she got a boyfriend, things were a little bit easier for a while, and she seemed happier. He left though, and every new boyfriend Mom got was worse than the last. She always liked to drink, but Booster got her interested in drugs and then she wasn't even Mom anymore. It was like she was just a paper doll where my mom used to be. She wasn't happy or sad or mad or anything. She was there, but she wasn't *really* there. Do you know what I mean? I don't want someone like Booster to come to your house and turn you into a zombie like my mom. She used to be pretty cool sometimes, but that was a long time ago. If I'm here, maybe he'll come back. He's mad at me, and he wants Brianne. So if I'm gone, maybe he won't ever come here again."

Her heart broke for Liam as she listened. He was the protector of Bella and Brianne and now he felt he had to protect her from the nastiness in the world too. He had somehow gotten the idea into his head the he was a magnet for the torment and malice visited upon him and that removing himself from the equation would somehow armor the good people in his life against the misfortune that he carried around like a pernicious infection. Believing himself contagious, his only honorable choice had been to leave, to exit the stage, to isolate himself and his sisters from others as if they carried a plague.

Cate discerned sturdiness in him, as strong and true as a redwood, and was astounded that such a child had sprouted from the environment he had escaped. She wished that he could see himself as she saw him, for he would never again question his worth if he could. This man-child was meant for greatness, and she knew, in that moment, that she wanted to be around to watch him grow into the man he would become.

Hannah stepped into the living room, handed him a cup of cocoa, and exited again without a word. Cate returned from her lapse into contemplation and wondered how to approach Liam without backing him into a darkness he could not escape. He was vulnerable, fragile, but even though his previous experience warned him not to trust anyone, he was risking his very survival and baring himself open to her, and she recognized that he could be shattered. She did not trust herself enough with words, so she reached out to him and drew him into her embrace. She held him, and they both wept in silence— he, longing for someone else to shoulder the burden, and she, out of allegiance to the welfare of this trio of lost children. She sat holding him in complete silence for over an hour. She allowed him time to cry it all out. She gave him time to extinguish the silent rage and confusion and doubt dwelling deep within his being.

At long last she spoke. Softly, tenderly, she whispered, "I'm going to be your rock. I'm going to be the person that makes absolutely sure that you and your sisters are okay. I will be the one that you can come to with any problem or concern, and we will work it out together. I will be the one who loves you no matter what. I promise you that there will be other people in your life as you grow that will cherish you. You already have Hannah and Frank on your side. Karen and Nobie are looking out for you too. We will all band together, and when trouble comes to follow you, next time, we'll be ready to help you out and then it won't seem so difficult to bear. We will all help you carry your load."

He pulled away so he could study her face, look into her eyes… and he believed her. He smiled and squeezed her arm. He felt lighter than he had for months.

She smiled at him and asked, "Shall we go try some of that French toast? I'm famished." She swung her arm around his shoulder, but this time, he grimaced and shrank back from her touch. "You're hurt." She was concerned. "Take off your shirt. Let's have a look at your shoulders." He didn't comply at first but reminded himself that he'd made the decision to trust her, so he slowly removed his shirt and turned to reveal his back. There were welts two inches thick all over his back and shoulders and a few wrapped around to his ribs. Some were open and raw, some were old and scarred over. "Did the medical staff examine these when Karen took you there?" she asked, appalled by the damage.

"I didn't tell them about my back. I just showed them my eye, and they took X-rays of my face to make sure nothing was broken.

I hid my back. I don't know why. Just didn't want anyone to know I guess."

"I can't believe you've been living under this roof, and I never noticed the pain you've been in. We should have someone check this out for you to make sure it doesn't get infected."

"Please don't," he pleaded. "I don't like the way people look at me when they see it. It'll heal by itself. It's happened plenty before, so I know, and it's already much better."

She considered his appeal, weighed his reasoning against her own worry and relented. "Okay, but I get to check it every night before bed to make sure it's healing, and I'm going to pick up some salve to put on it, and you have to promise that if it's hurting, you'll ask me for some Tylenol. Plus, no more secrets from me or Hannah. Do we have a deal?"

"Deal," he responded and put out his hand for her to shake, with a crooked little grin playing across his face that she had never seen before. She liked it. She took his hand and they shook on it.

"Now, what do you think about the firehouse tour? I told Nobie that I'd call him this morning if you felt like going, but we can always postpone if you're not feeling up to it. Should we go or postpone?"

"I think we should go. The girls were excited about it, and they never get to do fun stuff like that. I vote yes!"

"Okay, I vote yes," she was saying as they entered the kitchen where the girls sat with coloring books and crayons.

"What are you voting about," asked Bella. "I want to vote too!"

"We are voting on the firehouse tour. If you want to go, raise your hands."

Bella and Brianne were excited to see everyone had their hands up, and silly Hannah had both of her hands way up in the air. They were so excited that Hannah came around the island to help them down from the stools for fear of their falling right out of them. They danced and squealed and bounced all around the kitchen in anticipation. Cate gobbled down a couple of pieces of cold French toast and warmed her coffee with some from the pot. Hannah made Liam some fresh French toast and served them hot with syrup and butter. Cate picked up the phone and dialed Nobie to accept his invitation.

Then, when Liam had finished, she hustled the children off to their rooms to dress for the day's excitement.

She still needed to get dressed herself, but she grabbed Hannah by the arm and strolled into the living room. "Thank you so much for giving us the time to talk. It did me a world of good, and I believe Liam feels a little better too. I don't think I can let those children go. I'm not sure if there is anything I can do, but I need to talk to Karen. I wonder if there is even the slightest possibility of my adopting those kids. I believe we need each other. I have no idea of whether their mother would even part with them, but I'd like to try."

"I think that is a marvelous idea, and we won't know until we try. Imagine three children for Christmas. What could be better?"

The Christmas tree looked a little sad since it had been abused, but Cate decided she liked it. It would remind her of how blessed they were, how lucky they had come through the darkness together, and even though they all wore scars of one kind or another…wasn't that the whole point of the holiday season anyway.

About the Author

S hirley Wiggins is a single mother of two. She is a North Carolina native but moved to the Midwest as a young woman and has enjoyed living in the beauty of the north woods of Wisconsin and the lake shores of Minnesota. Having always had a love of reading, writing, and books, in general, she began weaving her stories during her college years and hasn't looked back. Having worked in the health care field for thirty years, she has recently retired which has enabled her to devote more of her time to writing.

CPSIA information can be obtained
at www.ICGtesting.com
Printed in the USA
BVHW082225080221
599628BV00001B/200